Captive
Audience

Captive Audience

Jessica Mann

David McKay Company, Inc.
Ives Washburn, Inc.
New York

CHAPTER ONE

Those whose tenure is permanent can afford to take a long view of university affairs. The undergraduate or the principal, due three years all together, must make a mark quickly, if at all. At Buriton university, the temporary incumbents had begun the spring term as they meant to go on.

The marchers turned into Armada Road while the senate was still on the first item of the agenda. Thea Crawford, bored by the proceedings, was gazing out of the plate glass wall of the senate chamber, and idly watched the students' unstately progress. They were in a friendly mood, unaggressive and enjoying themselves. The weather was mild; the resolutions of the beginning, and the examinations of the end of the academic year now equally improbable. The students pottered rather than marched up the hill, and stopped for some speeches on the mud scarred green of Freeman's Common to ginger up their aggression. From the senate chamber there was a bird's eye view and Thea wondered whether her husband, in his window across the road from the common, was watching also.

It was not a good time for energy. A resurgence of

ambition seems natural at the start of the academic year in October, after the long vacation. Now, in early January, Thea felt worn out by goodwill and extravagance, and the prospect of bad weather and hard work ahead; it was the doldrums of the year and should not, on the calendar, be its beginning; nor indeed was it for the matter in hand.

The senate agenda was almost identical to that for the last meeting of the Christmas term. Decisions deferred then reappeared for discussion now, and none of the professors had changed their minds. Nobody was less open to conviction than a scholar discussing administration, and the daylight dwindled as long-winded men reiterated their convictions.

Professor O'Connor persevered on his feet going through the figures unit by unit. Thea was not the only person in the room whose attention was obviously wandering, though the principal listened attentively, his dark, blunt face expressionless.

Why on earth did I come back after the tea-break to this damned meeting? Thea asked herself. But she knew the answer. Last year she had rarely attended committees and senates, preferring to concentrate on her department and her work; she was the professor of archaeology. This year, if she was not busy, she must go home to Sylvester. She wriggled uncomfortably, settling the heavy gown across her shoulders, ashamed to admit even to herself that she preferred this unprofitable episode to that alternative. She had nothing to contribute here, and was beginning to wonder whether she could offer anything more useful at home. She was not apt for nursing or for tenderness.

The senate chamber's windows framed a view of the little town with its enclosing hills, and the waters of the bay, calm and pink now, reflecting the light of the setting sun. From a window on the other side of the tower watchers could see the red ball sinking behind the Atlantic. Those members of the senate who were not concentrating on the matters in hand admired instead its rays glinting on the dome of the observatory, brighter than the beam of the lighthouse to the west of the town, which now began to sweep its regular pattern across the sea.

The students had finished their pause on the common for speeches. The foreshortened figures below appeared more active, agitated, perhaps belligerent. They marched without discipline but cooperatively, chanting. Thea rather enjoyed watching the demonstration, safely above it as she was. There were about two hundred students there, with three in the lead. It was very well timed. Posters on the campus, and messily duplicated leaflets scattered on the coffee bar tables had summoned demonstrators to assemble at half past three, and to be on hand for the climax at five o'clock. Out of the doors of the library, the arts and science towers, the canteens and cafeterias, groups of young people were now moving to join the crowd. Other people walked quickly past, dissociating themselves from the young.

In the middle of the modern blocks on the university campus stood the original house in whose grounds the new university had been constructed, dwarfed yet still dignified in its strange new company. In the past, the colleges and the elegant buildings in

7

the middle of the town had provided sufficient premises for a small university whose students came mostly from the West Country. Local gentlemen had educated their sons at Buriton, and a happy relationship existed between town, county and gown. Along with the changing buildings, the acquisition of land and the arrival of students from all over the British Isles, the relationship had changed, and now the campus on its hilltop was physically and emotionally independent. Instead of its centre being a pillared arcade of eighteenth-century buildings in Fore Street, the registry and offices were housed in this former merchant's residence whose grounds had been covered with modern towers. The elders of the town were not the only people who sometimes thought that this was a pity.

But in Fore Street several hundred students would not have had room to stand before the registry and shout; for now they were crowded together on the gravel sweep, some of them jumping down a six foot drop to the principal's lawn, some standing on the roof of the principal's car which was parked before the building. It was time for the office staff to go home, and Thea saw groups of typists and clerks leave, giggling at the students.

The chanting was loud now, and the words at last audible. They were calling, *Free for all, Free for all*, regularly and monotonously.

Inside the senate chamber discussion of the minutiae of money had been continued with what seemed to be admirable sang froid, though Thea was not the only professor whose interest was focussed outside the window. The aged professor of theology, rosy from sleep, looked anxiously from side to side, flustered by the unfamiliar noise.

The principal whispered something to the registrar, who got up from the seat and went out with a pile of duplicated papers from a table near the door.

The principal said calmly, 'Well, I think we have given that item a good airing. Shall we move on? Number three; the question of Freeman's Common is pressing now.'

'Excuse me, Principal.' The speaker was the sociologist, a bearded man with a northern accent whose speeches made his colleagues groan at their own folly in having appointed him. 'Aren't we being a little ostrich like? That's quite a demo going on out there.'

'Thank you, Professor Prothero. I don't think you need worry, we know that the students are committed to non-violence. An answer has been sent to them— the registrar is distributing it now.'

'But we don't even know what they're asking for!'

'It's something about a free-for-all they are chanting,' another man said.

'Today's demand is for unrestricted entry to the university,' Lewis Rochester said with a slight smile. 'I have had to inform them that it's not in our power to grant it. Our political masters—' he shrugged, inviting them to share his amusement.

The sociologist was incredulous. 'You don't suppose that will shut them up?'

'What do they mean by unrestricted entry?' Professor O'Connor asked.

9

'Open to anyone who wants to come, without exam qualifications,' the sociologist answered. 'It's not an original idea. Not a bad one either. I'm sorry, Principal, that your answer was so categorical. There is some sense on the side—'

'I'm sorry, Professor Prothero,' the principal interrupted him. 'We can't really discuss the matter now. It isn't open to this body to make such far reaching changes in our admission procedure, as you know, and that's all there is to it.'

'Anyway, how did you know what they wanted? You seem to have been rather well prepared, if I may say so, Principal.'

'Jabber, jabber, jabber!' one of the physicists rudely said. 'What's the point of gabbling on about it? I move the next item on the agenda, or we'll be here all night.'

'Well, I think you're all just fiddling while Rome burns,' Prothero muttered audibly.

'Talking of burning,' Thea said, opening her mouth for the first time in the afternoon, 'what's that smell?' There was a momentary silence in the room. Several of the senate members went over to the plate glass window and looked down at the crowd of students, who far from being calmed by the duplicated communication which the registrar had delivered had become wild and agitated. The rhythmic chant had degenerated into an almost frenzied screaming, and through it many voices could be heard calling 'Rochester out'. It was almost dark and the overhead sodium lights on the campus illuminated the scene.

The lights were out in the windows of the registry building; or were they?

Suddenly one of the windows in the front of the house, on the ground floor, blazed into orange light; perceptibly later followed the thumping sound of an explosion, and the noise of broken glass falling to the ground. Many of the students screamed, and those nearest the house pushed backwards, immobilised by the crowd.

There were thirty-five professors crowded together at the plate glass window watching the scene below, but it was many seconds before even one of them recovered from the shock to realise what must be done. And university telephone switchboards are notoriously slow in functioning. By the time the fire engines approached the campus, the flames had caught hold. Senior members of the university were down among the students, trying to make them disperse, but the inertness of mobs had prevented them from clearing a path, and some of the students, intoxicated by the drama, spread themselves in a chain to obstruct the access up the road, swinging their arms and laughing inanely.

Thea found, as so often when one participates instead of reading about something, that she could not really see what was going on. She was at the back of the crowd, wondering, indeed, whether she was not in the way and would do better to move off. But she was pressed in among the other people as the crowd surged backwards, and fire engines reached the gravel sweep. Flames were leaping through the roof of the old house by this time, and the heat was such that the students chose to retreat. The smell was, shockingly, agreeable.

Over the crowd's murmurs, the hiss of foam and water falling on to hot stone, and the windy roaring of the fire were loud. Thea was standing by now in the middle of a group of students whom she did not know.

'At least we weren't anywhere near it,' one girl said.

'No, they can't say it's our fault.'

'I'll bet they'll try though.'

'How can they? None of us was within yards.'

'Anyway, it's not all that easy to start a fire.'

'What does start fires, actually?'

'Electrical faults ...'

'Cigarettes in waste paper baskets ...'

'Overturned paraffin stoves ...'

'None of it sounds very likely here.'

'... Arson? ...'

Thea said to the girl beside her, 'What was happening when this began?'

'Nothing much. We were just milling around, you know.'

'We were chanting quite peacefully when suddenly there were these sirens—'

'We thought the principal had called the police—'

'Yeah—blatant provocation—trespassing on private quarrels—'

'Nothing to do with the fuzz—'

'So,' asked Thea, 'you tried to stop them?'

'Toby kept shouting about passive resistance—'

12

'That's right. We linked arms across the drive, it was all a giggle really—'

'Until they arrested some of the kids—and then we really got peeved.'

'They arrested some of you?' Thea said, shocked.

'Yeah, just like Trafalgar Square.' The youth who told Thea that sounded pleased. The implication was that the Buriton students had proved themselves, that to be carried inert into a Black Maria was an initiation ordeal now successfully endured on behalf of Buriton by a hero called Toby.

'Well, I hope you all get what's coming to you,' a furious voice said. Thea looked round to see the university's registrar beside her. The students she had been talking to stared blankly at him and edged away. The flames were dying down by now; flecks of soot and charred paper floated down and stuck wherever they fell.

The registrar was called Hubert Dale. Thea knew him because he had been a friend of her husband when they were at Oxford. But she would hardly have recognised his normally mild and diplomatic face as he grimaced towards the ruined building, frowning, with black streaks across his forehead. He muttered, 'Bloody young layabouts. That's the records of years gone in there—all my work since I came here. Vandals.'

'Surely—an accident—'.

'If you'll believe that you'll believe anything,' he said. 'Fine bloody coincidence, wouldn't you say, just the day they demand entry for anyone, to burn up all the application forms for next year—'

'But Hubert, there will be duplicates at the central registry.'

'They wouldn't know that. Destructive, mindless— there's no point in universities these days.'

Hubert Dale was the only person Thea could see who looked particularly upset. Many of the students had gone, and those who remained seemed almost cowed by the awesome end of an afternoon's marching. Hubert Dale pushed his way forward, and stood in front of the police car's headlights. His voice came powerful and angry. 'That's enough damage for one night. Now go home, all of you. Go along.'

The university registry had been almost completely. destroyed.

CHAPTER TWO

I had seen the fire from my bed; I had heard the swell of the noise, the progress from chorus to cacophony. The fire engines went past my window, followed by my neighbours on foot, and some late-arriving students. It seemed a curious reversal of roles for the Crawford family that Thea should be up there with the action while I stayed at home and worried about her.

I would have sworn, when I watched the students making their speeches on the common, that this rally was not the prelude to violence. Their unreasonable demand had been temperately argued in my earshot. And yet, what was my judgment worth? In a moment of frankness, Thea had said recently that I was becoming a manic depressive, affected to the point of amusement or disgust by my mood alone and projecting on to external events the aspect my own temper gave them; she tried, most of the time, not to agitate me. But what could worse agitate one whose reputation was founded on his power of being objective?

It is true that I was frequently depressed at the time, unless it would be more accurate to say that I was prey to a degrading self pity.

For I'm no longer the successful media man with influence emperors never wielded. I used to imagine myself as a puppet master manipulating the strings of the victims I interviewed, or a guru telling viewers what to think. Far fetched, I dare say, and conceited, too. I've got my come-uppance, or pride goeth before a fall, depending which idiom you prefer to phrase your clichés in.

Not that I ever really believed it, inhibited as I was by the remnants of puritan terrors: anything nice must be nasty, the kingdom of heaven won't be for the likes of me, rich men and needles' eyes, etc. You can't help your subconscious worrying even when the intellect rejects its anxieties. And even that sort of triumph palls. All the men I knew well who reached the top said that their success turned to dust and ashes. They had seen the frauds of fame and power. How biblical I'm being. I hadn't looked at it for years, until there was nothing else to read but the missionaries' gospel. I'll never disentangle those blood-thirsty sagas from my feverish distortions of them. Not that one could dream anything much worse; the prophets foresaw modern warfare all right.

I don't think that the citizens of this prosperous land have any idea what an island of peace they inhabit. This isn't the norm; no amount of donations to Oxfam will turn the rest of the world into the reasonable, civilised welfare states of north western European imaginings. This country is Johnny in the cartoon where everybody but himself is out of step. If there's a society out of place in this disordered

16

world it's the ordered one which we think everyone else should have. Is it crazy outside our tame-life reservation? Or are we evolving a new race, *homo pacificus*? More likely, we are lunatics behind bars who know that only we are sane.

I'm banging on again, as Thea would be too gentle to tell me; I watch the impatience rising in her eyes, and how she sweetens her voice, how she slows her breathing and forces herself to tolerance. She's kind, my God she's kind, and what an effort it costs her. She can't see far enough to be sharp or hasty: but a bit of bracing would be good for me in this slough of despond. What right, after all, have I to indulge in misery, pampered, cared for, comfortable as it's possible to be in my condition, when I've seen sights —but I won't start on that again. That's the dreadful thing about the rest of the world. Its sufferings become boring. You'd rather read and do something (I mean send a cheque, of course) for half a dozen juvenile or animal victims of a minor natural disaster, than be reminded of the universality of misery. Nature provides no such destructive elements as the human race.

Yet even knowing that, I had not thought aggressive the rally which I watched and listened to on the common. Granted that when I opened the window to hear the words I recognised the practised piano-forte, forte-piano of a rabble rouser, and I thought of what they would do if they were the people they thought themselves. I wouldn't be watching so dispassionately then. But there was no need to fear this lot, a straggle rabble; I watched and envied, but I loved them for being whole and healthy, unmaimed, unstarved, untortured; not a bandage or false limb among the lot of them. It is different elsewhere.

There were three leaders, two boys and a girl. They wore the faded uniform of their profession, and their persons displayed all the fashionable bony protruberances. Could it be that extreme sharpness of the pelvis and shoulder blades are another evolutionary modification of the human race? Even my lovely girl was stick-like in profile. She was distinguished by an immense smoothness of skin and hair and on those surfaces normally roughened by wear. Her lips, classic, pouting, sulky in repose, were matt and slick. They would feel like a lacquered finger nail if one stroked them, but they were not painted. Slippery, like an ice-cube; but warm, I suppose, so warm.

She had straight hair, glossy and brown, and skin which, if I were the other kind of journalist, I would call luminous—a peachy, light-reflecting cutaneous cover. Her eyes were dark—and of course, since she was then flawless, large and brilliant. Her name was Jenny Pascoe. She stood listening with that total relaxation of the facial muscles which in so many actors signifies an emotion too deep for visible expression: thought portrayed by motionless features, as the camera plots each flicker of an eyelash. She was watching the boy who was speaking, who was called Ian Macardle.

But the audience stared at the other boy and so, on and off, did the girl; and so, soon, did I. He was a magnet; he drew the gaze. And yet his face had two eyes and a nose and a mouth, no more, merely an instance of infinite permutations and combinations. Blue eyes, a straight, blunt nose, a full classical mouth, and fair curls, a suitable model for Praxiteles— meaningless in words, but as the stares of his contemporaries showed, most meaningful in the flesh. And yet, how rare. For Hitler and Napoleon were no beauties, and few other rabble rousers would make good photographic models. And this beautiful boy had them hooked simply by existing. While the ugly young man ranted and tiraded, the others watched the beautiful one to see whether to obey.

Ian Macardle was talking about social justice. 'They call it education,' he shouted. 'They cram it into us, facts galore, that they want us to spill on their exam books to judge us by. Is that education, I ask you, friends? We absorb their data, carefully processed, they don't want us to learn anything too dangerous, then they turn us out to apply it to the problems of big business, of the polluters, of their industrial friends. Well, OK, that's fine, big deal, but what's the content of the knowledge? It's stuff for cretins, for mindless bureaucratic, bourgeois artisans. OK, we accept that, we need it in the big wide world, but is this democracy? I—'

'You have full student representation, you can sleep with each other, have babies, have abortions— what more do you want, you bunch of lay-abouts?'

'I'll tell you what we want—we want all our friends to share all this.'

The other man drowned the approving roars again, yelling,

'What is there left to share?'

'Who, not what. We want this opportunity to be open to everyone—non-selective entry, a chance for every young person. Stop flinging them on the scrap heap at eighteen, stop judging everything by the ability to churn out bits of unrelated book learning. And that's what we demand. Toby, it's your turn.' He turned to the other leader with an expansive gesture.

Toby had been looking sea-wards, not at anything, that was clear, just resting his eyes on the blue distance but he turned towards the other students when Ian asked him to speak and he smiled with a sort of friendly benevolence. He couldn't have learnt the politicians' trick, it was a natural gift, but I'm sure each individual thought the smile was meant for him or her. His voice was unexpected by me though greeted by his audience with affectionate attention. It was plummy and old fashioned and would not have been out of place in a London club or an outpost of the Empire. One could see that he had been brought up with that accent and been too unselfconscious to teach himself another one. He was not the sort of person who was aware of himself, and now, when he spoke to about two hundred people, did so like an earnest seeker after truth in a small room with other philosophers. But they listened to every syllable as he mused, and grew calm as he preached Gandhi's message. They wouldn't have hurt a fly.

I was a radical student myself, before the days of violent confrontation, and campus politics, and I was only bored by Ian, not disapproving: I've heard it all so often before, whether articulate complaints in television studios, or playing at politics speeches by apprentice prime ministers, or the end of the line which youths like this don't know about, the words of riot-raisers, in other parts of the world than this. I've learnt to recognise the speech which will turn a peaceful morning into a bloodstained night, I know the boys whose unspoilt faces will be baton-pulped by evening. Riot-shielded police and soldiers throwing tear gas are no strangers to me. As I said, I've heard it all before. But this was something else.

I'd never heard a people-trap before. The only words for him are ruined by having been applied to men who never deserved them. But before football players, pop singers and politicians were described as having charismatic appeal, there was a word for people like Toby. I'll just say that he was a leader. If he had worn pied clothes and played a pipe, there would have been no students left in Buriton as he danced out of the town.

Not that what he said was very remarkable. I don't know if he had consciously transmogrified the teachings of his nursery, or whether he preached the New Testament thinking that he'd made it up. But leaving out any religious allusions, that's what it was, applied to mental wealth instead of material. It really did come down to that. Only the wealth he wanted to share was learning, and knowledge and things of the mind. He saw intellectual goods as a kind of riches which could and should be shared out equally, not stuff to hoard. So the corollary was that the possession of such wealth did not make one person better than another, merely luckier, and the poor in brains—or exam qualifications—had a right to part of it. He said that the kingdom of heaven would be closer to the intellectually meek; and none of the students even flinched. I think it was because he meant it all, and because he didn't want anything for himself. He proclaimed the supreme importance of the individual, of the human personality, while at the same time being obviously indifferent to his own. It was the others he wanted to make free. He was hardly aware that he existed himself, the total extrovert.

I saw the two boys as the visionary and the practical man. The girl was the inevitable hanger-on. She was an idealist, a hero worshipper. Yet Toby whom she adored looked like an unphysical man. After all, one needs a minimum of self-awareness to realise the attraction of someone else.

So what about the third of this curious trio? He didn't watch Toby with the same adoration that the girl and the other students displayed but it wasn't a face that was easy to read; I don't think he was hostile, rather indulgent perhaps, like a worldly man looking at a saint; with the calm certainty of one who knows that he is necessary to grease the wheels of an imperfectly revolving world.

The tableau is sharply etched in my mind, stringy, skinny figures against the limpid Cornish sky. My bed was angled to the window, and the window at an angle to the slope of the hill, so that if I leant back I saw foreground and far ground, but I had to sit up to see the middle view of the road and its flanking terraced houses running down to the shops and then to the sea. Denimed, admittedly, and urban, it was like a painting of Calvary.

Thea brought home later a copy of the reply the students received from the university authorities; apparently forewarned, they had armed themselves.

The letter was headed with the university crest and copied on a machine which made the words look hand-typed and hand-signed. It was in the form of an open letter to the students, and ended *Yours very sincerely, Lewis Rochester, Principal.* It took the form of a careful, simple explanation of the constitution of this or any other university, describing how decisions were made, and concluding that it was not in the power of the senate or the council or the court or even the full convocation to make the changes which were proposed. It suggested that those who felt strongly should make representations, as voters, to the government. The matter was factually stated and not patronising, but irritating, I dare say. I didn't much care. I had already lost interest by the time the last student moved off. Free sideshows were all very well, even when the form they took were watered down versions of what used to provide my bread and butter. But I tired quickly, and by the time the last banner waving student trudged past I was sunk again in apathy and in that exhaustion which is not cured by sleep. Once I was zestfully enthralled by the world and the interlocking curiosities of human existence. I reported on what interested me; and that was everything. But now I couldn't be sure that it was just illness making it all seem weary, stale and flat. I felt that disillusion had been creeping up on me; perhaps

I had not recognised, in the business of life, how my involvement had become automatic, how I investigated things because I had become educated to do so and no longer because in myself I desired to know the truth. It became meaningful, not deplorable, to say, 'It will all be the same in a hundred years,' or 'What difference will it make when we're dead?' ... but I was an idealist once.

Certainly when I went out to the East I was not aware that my own attitude had changed. I intended to report there on what I found with the same eagerness and truthfulness which had brought me to the top of my profession here. I liked, by the way, the things that went with the position; it is fun to be a public figure. But I'd done the job for the love of it, *credit qui vult*. I was glad when Bernard Trent offered me that new assignment, and thought, with conceit and pride and I think a certain sense of public duty too, that I would do it well. New lights, Sylvester Crawford lights on different angles of uncomfortable truths were what I wanted to give and what the public wanted to receive.

I had never been to the Far East before. I thought, before I went, that I knew what to expect. But I was wrong. And one can't believe that it will all be the same in a hundred years, when one sees the ruin and destitution which most of the world's fathers will leave to their sons.

No doubt time would have deadened my reactions. But I had only been away from home for a few months in the clamouring East, when I woke up in a hospital ward, a crowded, prayerful, Canute-like place, where

24

calm sisters of mercy did a good best for as many patients as they possibly could, and where the pavements and gutters of the neighbourhood harboured the rest. I wasn't left there long. The unjust fate which singles out my like for good fortune ensured that, as always, my experience of the common lot should be limited. Soon they took me to an American military hospital and set the miracles of modern medicine to work for me; and then they brought me home.

Thea lived, by this time, in Buriton. When I went off to the East she moved to Cornwall as professor of archaeology, and our son Clovis started at a weekly boarding school here, and after initial difficulties which caused me as much amusement as anxiety when she wrote to me about them, she settled well into a new life. She was living in a women's college, which was not actually the twentieth century equivalent of banishing one's wife to a nunnery while one went off to the crusades, for it wasn't the chastity of the environment which prevented me from moving in with her but merely the flights of stairs. She did very well for me at short notice.

We are in a small pink house at the end of a small Regency terrace, in a street running up the hill from the main street to the university. There are palm trees and flowering shrubs. Our neighbours are prosperous and genteel; they keep their houses painted prettily in pastel shades, they prevent their dogs from fouling the footpaths and their children from kicking their footballs at each other's windows. Our house has charming details of domestic design, in the form of its door handles and moulded cornices and a chim-

ney piece with dancing nymphs on it. The two downstairs rooms were thrown into one by a previous owner
and I sit in what was the dining-room and is now a
family sitting-room. It has a slow-burning french
porcelain stove, a long table for my books and tape
recorder and anything else that can be thought of to
cheer me up. Thea provides me with freesias, to take
my mind off the old blood and corrupt flesh which
poison my memories. And I sit or lie in the bay
window. I can aim the brass telescope at the ships
in the bay, as the old chap who died here used to do.
We took it over with the house. Or I can focus on the
life, busy by Buriton standards, in the main road at
the bottom of the hill. I am part of the neighbourly
scene. People nod and smile as they pass, call up
comments about the weather and deliver magazines
and home-made cakes. Everybody is very kind.

At the other end of the room is the kitchen. Thea
had it made by a sympathetic builder in time for my
arrival. Everything is within my reach so that I can
have cups of coffee while she is out; and in the
evening she potters efficiently and chats, while I can
watch her and feel the liveliness of her activity in
the room.

I'm getting better; the doctor says that I am healing.
It is my mind that is still sick. I cannot forget what I
have seen and heard and smelt; I drug myself with
temperate novels. There are piles beside my couch of
Trollope, the Bronte sisters, George Eliot, Mrs
Gaskell, and whatever Thea chooses from the library.
But still I'm haunted. I used to marvel at the Spanish
Inquisition; my generation disbelieved the cruelty of

the Nazis. But in my mind now rise the phantoms of the victims I have seen. What is humanity, that we treat men like beasts? There is a new four letter word in our vocabulary, the word applied to people by people when they slaughtered them like beasts. Gooks, they called them, less than human, and their consciences did not prick. I vomit at the very word.

What have we made of ourselves, that we match against eternity a time so cruel?

But I try to force such thoughts from my mind. Concentrate on the students out there, the sprigs of western civilisation. The beast is buried deep in them. I did not even believe them capable of setting fire to a building. Yet from my couch I saw the flames leap to the sky, and heard their cracklings and hisses. The fire engines and police cars went past my window, the smell entered through it. You might think that the events up the hill would have agitated me, immobile and unable to take part. It must have been a symptom of my condition that I was aware of the fire and unexcited by it, and that when Thea came in, I was dozing.

Another kind of woman would have said, 'Moping again?' and brightly drawn the curtains and made tea and poked the fire and plumped the cushions. Thea came and sat at the end of the sofa. She moved my leg aside, not with any particular care or sympathy but as though it were a heavy book or something else I would not be needing for the time being. I saw the clouds, reflecting yellow from the street lights, wind-whisked across the dark sky, and then she leant across me to switch on my lamp and all I could see in the window was her own vital figure and mine, hollow eyed and still. We looked like that in my mind's eye, too.

She drew off her gloves, finger by finger, and blew on her hands, rubbing her palms together. 'To think they say it doesn't get cold in Cornwall,' she remarked. She picked up the paper which I had been not reading all day. It was a good number; under Bernard's editing, it improved every week. He had not replaced me in the Far East, and there was nothing which should have given me a pang and indeed it didn't. Perhaps that was why I could not bear to read it. I did not like to realise how little I minded. It seemed distant and unnecessary. I said,

'Exciting day?'

'Mmmm.' She looked at me, anxious for a moment. I wish she wouldn't be so tactful. I'd be glad if I could feel what she thinks I'm feeling, jealousy for her professional involvement. If only I could see her as Thea, my wife, a half of our whole. In watching my life as it were from six feet away, in being always spectator more than participant, I am the captive audience of a very boring play. Along with my mobility, I seem to have lost my emotions. Though I liked looking at her. A very pretty woman, and more so these days, though whether that was the mild western air or the job, or merely in the eye of the beholder, I could not say. She has black hair, smooth and longish, and Wedgwood blue eyes of startling size and curiously undefined as though they are always filmed with tears. Her voice is incisive and low pitched, like the statutory woman on a serious radio

28

discussion programme. She probably makes her students tremble. I said, to show her that I was not enviously brooding,

'I watched the demo today.'

'I thought you would have.'

'Very dramatic.'

'What more can one say?' she asked.

'It was burnt to the ground, was it?'

'The shell of the house is standing. It was granite, very durable. But the roof has fallen in, and most of the inside must be destroyed. It's a horrid sight, actually. I've never seen a fire like that before.'

'Arson?'

'The police seem to think so.'

'Not the usual result of one of the students' fully frank and fearless dialogues, would you say?'

'Well it's not how most demos end, I admit.'

'I wonder whether they really did—they didn't look so rabid when I saw them.'

'You can talk to Hubert about it. He's on his way. He can't possibly do anything there yet.'

Thea often produced visitors in this rabbit-from-a-hat way these days, only too obviously with the intention of taking my mind off things. I have been interested, as the phrase goes, in people.

She got up, and without apparent speed but most efficiently did what she called getting the place organised. The room looked ready and welcoming in the time it took me to get to the bathroom and back. Thea had converted the little room under the stairs, once, I suppose, the study, into a bathroom full of the necessary appliances for an invalid. I could hear her clattering saucepans in the kitchen next door as I struggled with them. I paused, clutching the newel post, in the hall on the way back. There was a pretty curved stair leading out of the hall. I could see as far as the window in the back wall of the house, bubbled original glass set in the old astragals, because when the nineteenth-century owners showed the neighbours that they could afford plate glass they hadn't bothered to match it up at the back. I had never seen upstairs. Thea had described a first floor drawing-room with three floor to ceiling windows and little wrought iron balconies. I should, she promised, sit up there in the spring beside her window boxes full of hyacinths. She tried very hard to surround me with sweet smells. I don't think she was terribly worried about my physical wounds, which she had been assured that time was healing under my plastic carapace, but she had been much affected by my once telling her of the sick stink always in my nostrils. She knew a little what I meant, having suffered from sinus, and pitied me the more for it.

I heaved myself back to the bed, and watched Thea delicately chopping green peppers and tomatoes. Two saucepans were already bubbling and there were drinks out on the table with cheese straws and olives. She had put out a stoneware pot full of daffodils and pulled the sofa round so that I could watch her work.

Hubert came after we had eaten. He was frozen and furious, and Thea welcomed him with whisky. He was the one friend I had in Buriton before arriving here. We had not met for years, but we took up the relationship where we had left it off in Oxford many years before.

Hubert had dropped in when I first came, but I was too depressed or ill to feel the enthusiasm I would normally have felt at seeing him again; and he had been perceptive enough to go away unoffended. We had been close friends, and my picture of that Oxford life was predominantly of him and myself and a man now dead walking miles, hands in pockets, thoughts wide ranging, discussing those topics which seem, after that age, so time wasting, so useless to consider since their conclusions are not susceptible to proof: life, death and eternity.

Fifteen years on, Hubert had changed, from the wild to the materialist. His profession was not, as he had intended, that of philosopher. Far from it: he worked in university administration, he was the practical man taming the fancies of unworldly thinkers, bringing their crazier thoughts down to realities of money and politics. He represented a statistical average, with a wife, a mortgage, three children and two cars; he was a churchwarden, a member of the district council, the Parent Teacher Association, the local Historical Society and the Rotary Club. I was more pleased to rediscover our friendship than I can describe.

Now he marched the room restlessly, and when he came to the street end he lifted the curtain and peered up the hill.

'There's nothing you can do,' I said.

'I know. The police virtually packed me off. They're taking it seriously.'

'No doubt of arson?'

'Too soon to tell, they said.'

'It didn't seem a likely accident,' Thea said.

'I don't know. Anyway, they go through the motions. Something about sending samples to a forensic laboratory.'

'They find out where the blaze started,' I told him. 'There are often traces of what was used. Petrol, or jelly, or Co-op mixture, or something.'

'What—?'

'A do-it-yourself explosive. That's what they call it in Ireland.'

'Well,' Hubert said, 'I suppose there isn't much future in speculating. No doubt we shall face all the usual protests if the students are so much as questioned.'

'But Thea said that some of them were arrested.'

'That was just for obstruction. I expect that the principal will be down there giving evidence of good character and getting them off with a caution first thing in the morning. They won't care about that— be proud of it more likely.'

'What's he like? The principal, I mean,' I asked. 'He's in a rather embarrassing position, wouldn't you say?'

'Yes. But I wonder if he minds. We tremble before him, you know. Not a bit what we're accustomed to. His predecessor was old Myles, the historian, a dear old chap, so vague and benevolent, nobody could bring himself to demand anything. He was too soft a touch, no fun in striking belligerent attitudes if they're aimed at a latter day Septimus Harding. You couldn't make out a good case for yourself as a victim of bullying oppressors.'

'It could be a clever technique.'

'Yes, if one did it on purpose, but I don't think Myles did. And it's not the sort of attitude which one can see Rochester imitating very convincingly.'

'It doesn't sound as though you like him.'

'I don't dislike him. He's good at the job, as it happens. And it may simply be a coincidence that the student activists have coincided with his three years. But he tends to be rather high handed with my department. He sees himself very much as the boss. And of course when he makes deals or concessions about things like student participation it's I and my staff who have to deal with it.'

'What do you have to do?'

'I oughtn't to tell you, if Thea hasn't.'

'Not for publication, I assure you.'

'Ah well ... it involves duplicate meetings, that's the real trouble. A great time waster. You see, Rochester is a law-and-order man, standing firm, sending down trouble makers, all that, you know? Well, public opinion changes pretty fast about these things. Just now it's rather anti-student.'

'I've noticed. Expressions of considerable venom on the spectators' faces, I'd say, when they see the young at play.'

'Yes, well, when Rochester took over, a couple of years ago now, we were in a phase of most people being on the students' side against arrogant authoritarians. So Rochester trimmed his sails. In fact, he gave in, or persuaded the senate to give in. Oh, it may have been necessary, it may, come to that, have been right. I don't feel strongly about the rights and wrongs of it, though the whole thing is a nuisance. At the moment it means that we have the formal meeting with student members of committees and participants and observers from the students' union— all that. But unless they want what we want they get outvoted every time, because the senior members have met the day before to decide what they'll say and how they'll vote.'

'Don't they notice? The students, I mean? It must strike them as a bit fishy on occasions.'

'Oh, you'd be surprised how smart these academics can be,' Hubert said, with a sort of adult tolerance. He seemed to view the members of the academic staff of the university as his rather unworldly, childish charges, as though he were a kind of human sheep dog. 'No, the committee members argue and disagree with each other quite convincingly. It's a confidence trick which has so far worked—but of course the whole thing is a thundering bore.'

'I see that this illusory participation hasn't satisfied them though.'

'As a matter of fact, it worked very well until today. We've had various confrontations, as they call them; grants, you know, and the price of meals, and that sort of thing, and I must say, Rochester has handled them impeccably up till now; just the right combination of discussion, and independent inquiries, and concessions—he managed to get the wind from their sails very smartly. I'd not expected him to be so diplomatic. Of course, this would have been almost the

34

last fling, though I don't know what will happen now. What with exams at the beginning of next term and prospective employers coming round. The most scruffy of our activists tend to blossom out in dark suits come April.'

'Plus ça change ...'

'Yes, it's exactly what we did, isn't it? I don't know why they make me feel so intolerant now. I suppose it's because we're the wrong age, old enough to feel threatened by them, and not old enough to think of them as sons.'

'I don't feel threatened by the students I've so far seen. Though you have some interesting ones here. What about that Apollo of the soap boxes I saw today?'

'Oh, dear old Toby.' Hubert's face creased into a smile. 'Yes, he is different, there's no denying. But he'd be unusual in any generation. Though I suppose, until the last few years, he wouldn't be at a university like Buriton.'

'Oh?'

'Couldn't get into Papa's old college, I'm afraid. It was stretching a point to take him here, his A levels weren't up to much, but he charmed them at his interview. And of course even learned Englishmen like lords.'

Thea said, 'Hubert, do tell us more about the principal. He'd be a good subject for Sylvester, don't you think?'

'Really? Our Lewis? I suppose you can't keep yourself from analysing people. Many's the time that I've been glad I wasn't one of your victims, I can tell you. Though you're a pleasure to watch at work on other people. I'll never forget that time you wiped the floor with the Home Secretary.... But I guess our Lewis is the most interesting victim we can scrape up, down here. And there's his wife, of course—but you probably know all about that.'

'No.'

'Hasn't the gossip got round to Thea then? Oh, Joyce is a very lively figure round the town. She's a business woman. She ran a typing school, I think, before they moved here. That's what fed them, while Lewis was at the Bar. Then they moved down here and she started up a factory, making plastic toys. She's a real little ball of fire, tiny, you know, with red hair and a bit of a Scots accent. Comes from Glasgow, I think.'

'Plastics?'

'Yes, clever of her. I don't know why nobody had thought of it before. She utilises the waste products from the oil refinery. And she can always get labour in a place like this, there's nothing for people to do in Buriton except wait for the tourist season. The port and refinery are a bit too far to work over there every day. She gets her raw materials by sea, it's nearer as the crow flies, across water that is. And then she sends a good deal that she produces away by sea too, which eliminates one of the problems of local industry. Our land communications are so bad, that's the trouble.'

'She must be doing very well.'

'Oh yes. Lewis used to complain that his responsibility for her income tax took his whole income. They live in a quite unusual style for a provincial professor.'

'I've heard that they have a modern house.'

'It's a show piece, actually. The view from their windows ... Anyway, what Lewis earns even as the principal is peanuts to Joyce. I don't know why she bothers to stay with him.'

'Are they on bad terms?'

'I wouldn't be surprised. He's said to have an eye for the girls.'

'An occupational hazard,' Thea said drily.

'Does it matter?' I said. I was bored. It was nice to see Hubert, but we had little in common any more.

'I suppose there are plenty of divorced professors. But it's still frowned on a bit in some circles, especially if you leave a middle-aged wife behind and start afresh with a nubile student.'

'But he couldn't lose his job?' Thea said. Was she worried about the effect a woman professor's indiscretions might have?

'Not his chair, no. I shouldn't think they'd chuck him out of his college either. But I think that Lewis has his eye on higher things.'

'Like—?'

'Well, you know how we do it here; three year terms as principal, by election. I think he must be dreading going back to teaching law. It's not as if he's dedicated to research. His few articles smell of blood and sweat, I'm told, and there haven't been any for years. No, I think he wouldn't say no to a chance of running a bigger university. I'm told there's a big one in the north coming up.'

'The Northern University?' Thea asked, with interest. Academic gossip was more her line than mine.

Hubert took an innocent kind of pleasure in telling us about a meal he had had recently in the right club, surrounded by bishops and cabinet ministers, an establishment figure himself in this established world. He was showing off to me. I did not envy him the dull food and the careful conversation, but he was proud to have been in the right place to pick up the right gossip. He had drunk with vice chancellors and principals of universities. They were discussing the failure earlier in the week to appoint a new head of one of the big universities—a plum job in that profession, I gathered, which gave great power and influence, in a discreet way, to its holder.

The job had been lined up for a man I had heard of, a former civil servant who had been head of a small new university for a few years, and other candidates in the know had simply not bothered to apply. But Dick Milford had been unlucky. His little university had a phase of acute student unrest, and he had simply failed to control it; a fiasco for poor Dick Milford. So the appointments committee for the Northern University had politely turned him down; and having no other candidate for their hot seat—and this university was a nursery for agitators, even I had known that—they were holding the job in abeyance for a while. The place would be run by a committee of senior professors, poor chaps, and next time round they hoped to find a strong man. They were thinking unofficially in terms of a former colonial governor. I could visualise Lewis Rochester being interested in that sort of job, from what I had seen of him. Thea had asked him round during the vacation, to 'Take me out of myself', as I've no doubt she put it to herself. I remembered the day well, it had been one of my worst ones, and only the rigid habit of years had enabled me to mime good manners. It was the end of the day and Clovis had gone out to a pantomime. I had been relieved to see him go, and Thea was angry at my relief. She went to the door again to let Rochester in and they stood chatting for a moment in the hall. I could feel the cold wind rustling in the room. The papers flapped on to the floor and knocked over a wine glass, spattering my plaster with drops of claret. I was shivering when Lewis Rochester came into the room, ablaze with warm life, an enormous man who loomed above me, and fixed my eyes in the bright dark gaze of his own.

What would I have felt about him if I had been perfectly well? I should at least have been more detached. Now, I was frightened by the size and atmosphere of the man, a twentieth century and urban elemental. His gentleness was so obviously put on for me, a conscious control of his personality. I should have liked to have the cameras and lights, my usual protection, to chaperone us.

'I've long wanted to meet you,' he said, pumping my hand up and down. His voice was, surprisingly, transatlantic, a modified New England I thought, but his appearance was clubland, all pin-striped, pinhead dotted, navy blue. He was an enormous man, and when he sat on the bentwood rocker he looked enthroned. Thea, at any rate, didn't seem to be unduly impressed by him, and without lessening her usual informality she started washing the dishes at the other end of the room, and ground coffee noisily, and poured it into mugs.

I felt at a disadvantage, lowly reclined below Lewis Rochester. He was making conversation, talking tolerantly about the students' need to express their own personalities in protest. Thea mentioned an archaeologists' pressure group, and Rochester gently mocked the whole pressure group syndrome, and talked about the realities of power in a democracy.

I recognise ambitious men when I see them; the lust to power, or prestige, leaves a kind of Cain's mark on those who feel it. I asked him,

'You never thought of going into politics?'

'As a back bencher?' He was astonished. 'Good heavens no.'

'I don't think people start out intending to remain back benchers.'

'Ah well, my background is against me. Too trans-atlantic for the British and too British for the Canadians. No, my accent would create enmity. I need a non-elective office.'

'But you were elected to your chair of law, and to your present position.'

'Ah, universities are different. Positively xenophilic. You wouldn't find half the senates' names in a dictionary of English surnames. As for running the place, most of them regard it as a burden, not a privilege.'

'It seems to suit you.'

'Yes, I enjoy the work. I've always thought that if you're able in one field then you can be in all. It's only a question of applying the trained mind.'

'So you're an élitist.'

'I do believe that some of us are superior to others, yes. The concomitant, as I tell my son, is more responsibility than rights. One is very aware of one's duty to the community.'

'You have just the one son?'

'Yes, like yourself. It's a great pity, in both your case and mine. I really feel that the intelligent among us should reproduce themselves.'

'Shouldn't people like ourselves be sufficiently intelligent to limit their families?' I said.

'Oh no, my dear fellow. Think of the average ability of the human race. It's an elementary principle of social engineering that we need to provide the administrators of the future, the doctors, the inventors. The world needs more like us.' I knew that this was a view held very sincerely by many people more modest than Lewis Rochester. Why should confidence in his own worth and usefulness put my back up? And why should I cringe at the perfectly respectable sociological conception of social engineering—people planning as I had heard it called? But it offended me. I said coldly,

'Is this what you teach your pupils?'

'Implicitly, I believe. It's not the sort of thing one says in public, my dear fellow. Example, not precept, you know. But I think the message gets across. I've had some very clever boys, very successful. They do me credit. I built up a quite well known little law school here. Buriton law graduates are doing extremely well.'

'You must find that gratifying.'

'Yes, one takes a certain satisfaction in these things. Though one is merely doing one's duty as best one can.'

Rochester's virtuous emphasis on his duty to others was designed to make me regret that my ballroom-dancing parents had not been hot gospellers. I couldn't help wondering whether Rochester had got it quite right. He behaved like an able man and spoke like a public spirited one. Why did I think that it did not ring true? If at the time I'd had the energy, I would have disliked him, and later, talking to Hubert, I was surprised by the emotion the thought of Rochester aroused in me. I said, 'Are you interested in running a big university?'

Hubert laughed a little self consciously. 'I have sometimes wondered why they always think that scholars will do the job better than people who have run the blasted places all their lives. In the States they have professional administrators doing the job, not scholars drafted from their books and hankering for the class room for three years. Not that the present principal misses his lectures, though he's still the senior professor of law, you know; it's still his department, and he keeps tabs on the law students, I can tell you. But no, of course not. It would be way above *my* station in life.' I yawned and Hubert stood up. 'I think I'll just wander back up the hill. They should have had a chance to see by now ...' He left, promising to come again.

Thea chatted as she tidied the room for the night, and she helped me in and out of the chair with amazing strength for a small woman. 'Clovis will be back for the weekend tomorrow,' she said. 'You can finish the game of Monopoly you started on Sunday.'

'Our son's an embryo capitalist,' I complained.

'Good, he can support us in our declining years.' She kissed me briefly on the forehead. My God, my mouth wasn't in plaster, nor my hands. But I said, 'Good night darling,' and closed my eyes. I would not force her to kiss me if she did not want to. It was bad enough that she had to perform other distasteful chores on my behalf. I took deep breaths to calm myself and lay still until she left the room. It was better than the hospital. It was better than it might have been. I lay there willing myself to acquiescence, and listened for most of the night to the hooting of the buoy in the bay.

CHAPTER THREE

All over the world universities had become used to student unrest; in other countries it toppled administrations not only academic but even national. Yet in the British Isles moderation had survived. Sit-ins, take overs, marches, rent strikes, had been the greatest achievement of the young revolutionaries, and were beginning to be taken for granted, as a regular between-examination game. Many scholars relied on having a few days each term when they could get on with their own writing undisturbed, until classes were resumed. It was almost traditional that no punishments would be exacted, or if they were, either by civil or university authority, then the other would ignore it. Yet, as Thea found when she arrived at the campus the next morning, there came a point when enough was felt to be enough. Buriton had never seen paving cobbles torn up and barricades of overturned buses; had never even thought of riot police with clouting batons. This was England. And today the general feeling was that the students had taken advantage of kindness and tolerance; they had gone too far.

A meeting of the university staff had been called for the middle of the morning, and when Thea arrived, a little early, she found colleagues in angry or dismayed clumps. Professor O'Connor was declaiming to several of the younger lecturers in his department.

'It's time we clamped down,' he said. 'I've always known that it would end with something like this, giving them all that freedom. Students aren't ready to organise their own lives, they need to be taken care of. We simply evade our own responsibility if we pretend that they are adults just because some electioneering dodge gives them the vote at eighteen. Even twenty-one is too young. No, it's as I have often said, I knew we would be in trouble.'

'Yes, I know you have,' a younger man murmured. 'But it's nonsense, Alfred, you know that really.'

'What do you mean?'

'Well, not all student demos end in fires. We don't even know that they were anything to do with it—an old building like that could easily—'

'A fine coincidence that would be, I must say.'

'Well,' the young man persevered, 'I think they are mostly very responsible young people, far more mature than we were at the same age.'

'I don't know why you should say that. When I was nineteen I was fighting for my country—not bumming around at someone else's expense. What contribution do they make to society except to disrupt it?'

'Mightn't that be quite a good thing?'

'Oh—' Fortunately at that moment the principal

45

came into the room, and Alfred O'Connor stood smartly up, demonstrating old fashioned values to his subordinates. Lewis Rochester looked grave.

'Good morning,' he said, and was answered by a subdued chorus. 'I am afraid that I have more bad news for you,' he went on. 'You may have thought that the destruction of the registry was bad enough; I am sorry to have to tell you that the fire resulted in the death of one of our students who was in the house at the time.' He held up his hand to still the immediate whispers and gasps. 'His body was found in the remains of a small room, which he had apparently been using instead of lodgings.'

'Who was it?' called Alfred O'Connor.

'The body has only just been identified. It was not found until the early hours of the morning, when the ruins were sufficiently cooled to be thoroughly investigated. The student's name was Winston Simpson. He was in his second year, reading combined arts subjects.'

'But how is such a thing possible?' a woman lecturer in botany asked. 'I'm sorry, Principal, but what do you mean when you say that he'd been living there?'

'I shall ask the registrar to explain.'

Hubert Dale stood up, angry and bewildered, but still conscious of his own efficiency.

'You'll all know—or rather, knew the building. Some of you will remember it when it was still a private house. Well, it wasn't ideally suitable to convert to offices. It was before my time, but I know that my predecessor complained that it would be inconvenient and expensive as a registry. It rambled, and

46

wasted space. But of course, there was a conservation order, and we couldn't demolish. Anyway, that's a digression. The result was that we used all we could in the main body of the house, and we used a lot of the outbuildings for storage, files, and paper and what not. All gone, by the way, burnt to cinders. But that extension at the back, what had been the laundry and the dairy and so on, most of that was useless for our purposes. You'll all know where I mean, that sort of lean-to with slate hanging and windows one foot square. Well, to be accurate, in the ground floor part of it we kept odd things like a defunct duplicating machine, and spare coat racks and things for Open Day. But there was a staircase, more like a ladder really, leading up to what must have been a maid's room. A real slum it must have been, dripping damp, too; and they'd put a primitive bath into one corner for the wretched servants, practically a museum piece in itself. I'm going on about it rather, because I know it's hard to believe that one of the students could have used that as his living quarters for a whole term quite unnoticed. But you can see why none of us ever had occasion to go there. And it does seem that's what happened. You'll recall the fuss we had in the autumn about lodgings—well, we always do, every year; rows of them on the floor of the students' union and squatting in our offices. We thought we'd got them all fixed up in the end. But this boy apparently made himself a sort of snuggery, though his head must have hit the ceiling when he stood up. He slept in the old bath, by the way, in a sleeping bag. But of course nobody knew he was there.'

47

'Principal, I must protest,' Professor O'Connor said loudly. 'The registrar will have opportunities to defend himself if charges of negligence are brought at a later date. Our first concerns must be with the late Winston Simpson, about whom we have been told nothing. Has his family been informed? Which of our number was his moral tutor? We cannot thus let this tragedy pass.'

'I assure you, Professor O'Connor, nobody intends to let it pass. But the registrar was answering the question as asked. Winston Simpson seems not to have had a moral tutor; and that may explain how he managed to live at such an unorthodox address for so long.'

'Impossible!'

'No, I am afraid it is increasingly done,' the principal said. 'Now that the students have the right to change their moral tutors at will—a concession they won, you may recall, two years ago, against, I may add, my own advice, it is possible for them to break off relations with the tutor to whom they have been assigned without taking any steps to find a new one.'

'Disgraceful!'

'Does that mean that none of us knows anything about the boy?' a motherly looking woman asked. Thea recognised her as a junior lecturer in history, returned after twenty years of child minding to help out in her old job.

'We shall no doubt be asked that by the police,' Rochester said.

'My God—I suppose it's manslaughter.' Professor Prothero cried. 'It never occurred to me.'

'We don't know that,' Thea said. 'Have we any

reason to be certain that the fire was not accidental, Principal?'

'He could have started it himself,' another man added. 'Smoking or something.'

'Goodness, I remember him now,' a young woman said. Everybody turned to look at her; it was a young lecturer in philosophy, whom Thea had met in her own college, Anna Morgan. She blushed at the attention, but went on, 'You know how it is, you have these huge lecture classes and half of them don't turn up to tutorials—I'm sure some of the students spend three years here without ever actually meeting a teacher. But Winston Simpson—I saw him on the campus once. I don't know that I should—'

'I am sure that anything you can tell us will be very helpful.'

'All right, Principal, if you say so. Well then, he was high. Stoned. Paralytic.'

'Drunk?'

'No, drugged. I stumbled over him. Oh, you must all have seen them. Not necessarily here, but over in St. Ives, or on the beaches. Or in bus shelters. You recognise it when they're hopped up.'

'I am happy to say that I do not,' Professor O'Connor said.

'Well anyway, it was late one night, and his friends had dragged him out of the way, propped him in a passage against a wall. They are always awfully kind to each other, drug addicts, you know. Much more so than—'

'Miss Morgan, I am sure that we should be very interested to hear your views on the better natures of law breakers another time,' the principal said. 'If you could just tell us something now about Winston Simpson—'

'Oh sorry. Well, I saw him round the campus occasionally after that. I'd read his name on his books, that time I fell over him—anyway, he used to sort of shamble round. You know. I didn't really know him. Just to say hullo to sometimes.'

'You will have to tell the police about him,' the principal said.

Thea said quickly, 'Do describe him. Some of us might know—'

'Well, he wasn't unusual. Terribly thin, narrow really. Not very outstanding. Except he spoke so slowly, he had a sort of dopey voice—not that he ever said much that I heard. I suppose he must have been drugged all the time.'

'Did you know where he was living?'

'Oh no, Mr Rochester, I didn't know him at all. I don't even know if he was ever in my classes. All I meant was that I recognised the name.'

'Well, that doesn't get us any further. No doubt the registrar will get in touch with his—'

'With all my records gone up in smoke that won't be easy,' Hubert Dale said. 'But I'll find out through the colleges. I'll see to it, Principal, yes.'

'Thank you. Well, if that's all—'

'I'm sorry, Principal, it's not all. What about the fire? Who started it, and how will he be dealt with?' Alfred O'Connor was severe, but Lewis Rochester was very much in control, and spoke with authority.

'That's all I can tell you, I'm afraid. We must all

50

wait upon the police investigations. Until then, there's nothing we can do.'

The room emptied slowly; it had been agreed that classes and lectures were to be suspended, partly as a mark of respect for the dead student, partly as an expression of disapproval of the living students' behaviour, and partly to enable the police to get on with their enquiries more conveniently.

After an unsuccessful session with her secretary, Thea was stopped on her way to the car park by Hubert Dale and told that there was to be a private meeting of heads of department at the Rochesters' private house. He was angry, and cursed the idea of having to skulk where the students could not spy on proceedings. Thea was ashamed of her relief that she could put off going home a little longer.

It was cold and grey, but clear. A gaggle of students went by shouting at each other, and one of them called in a friendly way to Thea, 'Let off with a fiver for obstruction! Care to contribute?' They had a martyr for the cause, but no doubt the students' union would have a whip-round for the fines; well, she thought, fair enough. And there was Rochester, letting Jenny Pascoe out of the car; back from court, no doubt. A pretty girl hiding it as best she could with the ugliest clothes she could find, Thea thought, though Rochester certainly looked at her indulgently enough. He loomed over her, a different scale of human being.

Thea found herself following the principal's car in her own mini, up the coast road to his extraordinary glass-walled house. The door was opened by Mrs

51

Rochester, who showed the professors into a huge room, foam cushioned and brick floored; there were counters but no tables, all covered with stainless steel, and some self conscious bric-à-brac was displayed in strategic places. The heads of department arranged themselves on such seating as was available, and listened to Rochester's plans for dealing with the students. Thea did not attend very carefully. It did not sound very different from the usual plans she had heard so often since she started working in universities, no more likely to have the desired effect of achieving a pre-war obedience than any other. And the experience of one term had shown that Rochester always got his own way with his senate. They argued and disagreed and ended up by voting for what he wanted.

After a while Mrs Rochester pushed in a trolley of coffee, and they all stood sipping. Thea found herself admiring the view beside her hostess. 'What an amazing room,' she said politely.

'Yes, isn't it?' Joyce Rochester answered, bored. 'It's all the architect's idea, of course. He had a free hand.'

'But surely—your collections—?' Thea gestured towards some glass shelves set across the alcove beside the enormous stone fireplace. Joyce Rochester laughed.

'The Lalique? That was one of his ideas too. He said we had to collect something.' She switched on some concealed lighting, and the little clouded glass figurines and bowls sprang into translucent prominence. 'I'm not much interested in objects myself, but

I dare say they are suitable. And they have their uses —I have moulds made from them in the factory for replicas. They went very well this Christmas.' Thea, as an archaeologist, was interested in objects and found this obscurely shocking. 'I hope this isn't all going on too long,' Joyce Rochester said. 'I've got a friend—oh, there he is.' She went to the door again, and Thea watched through the glass as she greeted the man who had just come. She brought him into the room, and introduced him as Desmond Pascoe, a large, loose skinned man whose chin overlapped his collar and whose drooping eyelids almost hid his eyes. He accepted a glass of tomato juice and raised it, saying,

'Well, here's luck. I'll need it if Jenny goes on like this.'

'She escaped with a small fine,' Thea said.

'Till the next time. I don't know—these young people ...' he moved his shoulders slightly as though shrugging off that worry, and said to Thea, 'So you're one of these lady professors.'

Thea said, 'Are you connected with the university at all?'

'Not apart from having a daughter there. I'm just a business man.'

'Desmond is a building contractor on a huge scale,' Joyce Rochester said.

'Till I go bust. We're having a recession, remember.'

'Of course, one is protected from economic realities in my job,' Thea said.

'But you are bound to be part of them. Actually,

the university is one of the main creators of prosperity round here, being one of the biggest employers,' Desmond Pascoe told her.

'I'm afraid I'm very ignorant about that kind of thing.'

'Your mind on higher things no doubt, Professor Crawford. But take it from me, the university is a good thing for Buriton. Makes all the difference to the landladies, for instance, to have trade all the year round.'

'So you don't feel that there is a conflict between town and gown?'

'The students get a bit above themselves now and then, not least my Jenny. But they are only young once. You can't blame them all for yesterday's tragedy. I'm sure it was a pure accident.'

'There's a conflict over Freeman's Common,' Joyce Rochester said.

'I know it,' Thea said. 'We live opposite in fact. The university—well, perhaps I'd better ...'

'Oh that's all right, it's no secret that Lewis wants it,' Joyce said.

'Lewis wants to put another of his awful towers on it,' Desmond Pascoe said. 'We're at daggers drawn, with the council as the umpire. It's the council selling it, as you know, and granting planning permission to one of us. The advancement of learning against filthy commerce, isn't that right, Joyce?'

'Don't run yourself down,' she said sharply. 'He wants it for a very useful development, the sort Buriton really needs, offices, supermarkets, you know the sort of thing. A shopping centre. It'll bring the

54

prices down, and with all the old age pensioners we have here, as you've said, Desmond—he's a Samaritan, you know—'

'Yes, well, I don't talk about that,' he interrupted. 'But I would like to include a day centre for the old folks with lunches and bingo, you know the kind of thing.'

'Is it a private development plan?' Thea asked.

'Well, half and half. Amenities in exchange for cooperation. But of course it will come to nothing if Lewis persuades the council that his need is greater. It's the last land in town. All the hills around are scheduled to stay open land.'

'Who'll decide in the end?' Thea asked.

'The council. They'll choose between our rival schemes.'

'All you need is a few more demonstrations like yesterday's, Desmond, and the councillors won't want anything more to do with the university ever,' Joyce Rochester said.

'You're joking, of course,' Pascoe said, looking shocked. Thea liked the man. He spoke with earnest consideration, and had an air of ruthless benevolence, as though he would always act for other people's good, but knew best himself what was good for them.

'Yes, you old Methodist, I'm joking. Why are the virtuous so frequently without a sense of humour, have you noticed it, Professor Crawford?'

'Five minutes, Professor Crawford and gentlemen, please,' the principal called.

Thea asked for the bathroom, and was conducted to it through a tidy, functional bedroom. Mrs

Rochester showed her the plug, which was indeed unidentifiable, and said, 'You can find your way? I must just ...' and went hastily off. It was while Thea was sitting there, thinking that the paper must be in a logical place and that she was probably staring straight at it when she heard with disconcerting clarity voices nearby. Thea was neurotic about lavatories, only able to use a bathroom with a lock on the door and therefore rendered miserable at her friends' weekend cottages; she was inhibited to the point of blockage by the knowledge of ears within range. She sat paralysed.

That was Lewis Rochester's voice. 'I won't have it in this house,' he was saying, furiously and urgently. 'Nor in front of all these people.'

'You know what you can do about it then.' That slightly Scottish voice was his wife's.

'You know our agreement perfectly well. You promised you'd be discreet.'

'So did you. But really you know, Lewis, all these dreary people—using the house as an office—not a soul in the room I want to speak to.'

'I know whom you'd like to talk to. And not just talk to.'

'And not just like to either, my dear. I'm beginning to think that it's about time we gave up this farce though.'

'You know perfectly well that he doesn't want a scandal just now any more than I do. Or than you do, Joyce.'

'Och, I don't mind so much. They won't stop buying my plastics because they're made by a loose

56

woman. My morals don't come into my job the way yours do.'

'He cares about it though.'

'Yes, though it doesn't matter quite so much for him. I'm not sure he wouldn't like to go in with me.'

'What—go over to plastic manufacturing? How could he? The firm—'

'He'll need a big contract to make it worth keeping on just now. Trade's been very slack—they may have to lay off some men. And all that bit about his local position, I'm not sure he wouldn't trade all that for me.'

'And his wife? I thought—'

'Oh well, nothing's settled. But don't you be so sure of yourself. You should be grateful to me for not just going, and to him. But he'll need some more inducement at this rate, or there won't be any point in it for him. You know, if he could . . .'

'Shut up about it just now, Joyce. It's nearly over and you did promise.'

'I suppose I was ass enough to feel sympathy for you.'

'Was it really only that? We can hardly go into it now, but I'd have thought—'

'Look, while you were a law teacher, or even a barrister, that was one thing. OK, so I'm not madly interested in it, but I can see the point of the subject, I use the services of lawyers in my business, it's got some function in the world. But this crazy ambition you've got now of running universities— I mean, who cares how they run? You know perfectly well that anyone who is the least bit realistic thinks that the crowd of layabouts you spend your days pampering should be out digging drains or doing something useful. If you want me to go on taking part in this farce so that you can make it your life-work, speed it up a bit, that's all.'

'I didn't realise you felt quite that way about it.'

'Am I hurting your feelings? But you hurt mine, with this cold blooded assumption that I'll deprive myself of what I want in life so that your reputation won't be sullied, yours of all people—'

'But wouldn't you like it? The position, perhaps a title—'

'Look, mate, you can have your fun being a big time organiser, the boss man, whatever you like, but you've got the wrong sort of wife to thrive in your shadow. I don't care about your worldly position or power—it's mine that matter to me, and I'm simply a business woman. I just don't care about the world you live in, it's meaningless to me, can't you see that?'

'Most wives care for their husband's sakes.'

'Oh, Lewis. For heaven's sake.' Her voice sounded pitying. 'Please don't kid yourself, my dear. We haven't properly been husband and wife for years. And whose fault is that? You go and find yourself the usual consolation.'

Their voices faded away, and Thea found a paper tissue in her pocket and was able to leave the little room.

She felt, and later laboriously tried to define, a curious mixture of sensations, once she had put aside her shame at having eavesdropped. In many ways

58

she admired Joyce Rochester for making a stand about living life as herself and not in her husband's shadow. Yet was it quite fair? In our world, she thought, it is simply a fact, deporable or otherwise, that a husband's job is affected by his wife's behaviour. Was this something one accepted on marriage —part of the deal? It was the rare couple for whom it could be a question of give-and-take, for few women's careers demanded more than tolerance of her husband; none, she thought, except the Queen's, active participation. So was she sinning against her own principles about feminine freedom, when she thought that Joyce Rochester was behaving like a bitch? Did Lewis deserve that she should feel sorry for him? An odd couple; an odd set up. And when the meeting was finally over Joyce Rochester and Desmond Pascoe reappeared in the big room, and Joyce Rochester was almost overwhelmingly friendly and cordial to Thea, referring many times to the pleasure of at last having a woman on the senate of the university, and of the excitement Sylvester's presence had created in the town. She looked flushed and untidy; as she spoke, she moved a sticky eyelash from the corner of her eye with a sharply scarlet finger nail. She looked sexy and unacademic, and not entirely clean.

Thea described the occasion to Sylvester when she got home. He liked it, she thought, if she told him about the world outside, and he used to say that she had a talent for doing so, for she had no imagination and the archaeologist's photographic memory. However, little as she was in the habit of examining motives, she had found both the Rochesters' extreme friendliness rather strange.

Sylvester laughed. 'You are naive, darling. Think: you've seen this before.'

'What do you—oh, Lord. You think they want to get at *you*?' In London Thea had become used to being cultivated for her husband's sake. She was quick to recognise the man—it was usually a man— who hoped that she would tell Sylvester Crawford what a fascinating person she had met and how well worth an interview he would be. Recently she had lost the habit of remembering that she was an influential man's wife.

In Buriton for the last eighteen months she had been an entity herself, a new and successful professor establishing her department and her home out of Sylvester's shadow. She had enjoyed it, she suddenly, guiltily realised, until he came. But she had always hated looking after people who were ill, even her own child. It would be all right when he was better.

'Did I tell you there have been several calls today? People asking what's going on,' Sylvester said.

'What, the national papers? And the BBC?'

'I can't think why you're surprised. It isn't exactly a normal event, what happened yesterday. Bernard rang to ask me to do a piece.'

'Will you?'

'I shouldn't think so. You're the one that cares about Buriton; I'm only camping here.' He picked up *Jane Eyre* and started reading; Thea's lips tightened as she glanced at him, and then she went over

to start the supper; bangers and chips, because Clovis
was coming, and this, whatever Sylvester implied, was
home.

CHAPTER FOUR

When they left me alone I was sorry for myself. When they tried to help I felt badgered and beset. Saturday was a bad day.

At least Thea never stayed whispering in the hall with the doctor. If she had private conversations about me with him on the telephone from her office, I did not know about it. In hospital, it is not pain but ignorance, that is unbearable. For twenty-four hours I thought I was dying, before the sister could be induced to explain to me the admittedly disagreeable but not fatal multiple fractures of a varied selection of my bones.

Thea brought Tim Gifford in, saying to him loudly that all I needed was pep pills, and I did not detect any conspiratorial glances between them. He had come to take the regular blood sample, to check on my prothrombin level.

After the setting and plastering of my broken bones I'd nearly died from a blood clot. I had to keep still and take pills to make sure that it would not happen again; but it did not hurt. Tim sat heavily down and flicked my plaster legs lightly with his nails.

'Not much for me to look at,' he remarked.

'No, but it's nice for me to see you. Are you in a hurry?'

'If you mean will I have a drink, then I've time for that.' He sat sipping peacefully, quite unlike the traditional picture of the Health Service practitioner rushed off his feet. He looked more like a farmer anyway, red face, untidy, thick white hair, shaggy clothes. He had the knack of seeming to know his patients well after brief acquaintance, but I felt that he really did like Thea and me. Was this keeping me company by way of medicine? I did not think so. He said abruptly, 'You can't go on like this, Sylvester, can you?'

'Like this?'

'Oh, you're healing up, I don't doubt, under there. You'll walk again. But you'll be off your head before then; can't you write a book or something? It's exciting enough round here for one. Or give tutorials to some students? I'd have thought one could be a journalist quite well from a sick bed.'

'I do write the odd article and book review.' I was on the defensive; there had been a pile of new political volumes sent by the literary editor of my paper on the table beside me for days. Having no deadline, I couldn't be bothered to start.

'Not enough. It's bad for you to have so much thinking time. A man like you needs to be working. Look—' he ran his finger over the keys of my typewriter and it came away grey, 'I can see when you last touched this.'

'"When my daddy works he just sits" is what my

63

brother's child once said,' Thea remarked. 'He's a philosopher, of course.'

'Yes, well, sometimes I sits and thinks and sometimes I just sits,' Tim said. 'Me, I just sit. But then I'm offensively healthy and I'm not the brooding type. I'll stick the occupational therapist on to you if you go on like this, old chap. If you'd stayed in hospital they'd have made you weave baskets, you know that?'

Thea was standing at the kitchen end of the room and she winked at me over Tim Gifford's head. 'I'll set him a course of improving reading,' she promised. 'Wean him off those interminable Victorian novels. But lay off the poor chap, Tim. I'll think of something.'

'Well, see you do, my girl. I don't approve of drugs to pep up perfectly sane people like your husband here. It's natural to mope in the circumstances. But we let you come home because you said you'd be happier, old man. So prove it. I'll look in again on Monday.' He went out, waving jauntily from his car. Thea looked at me sympathetically.

'I suppose we do like him,' she said.

'He means well.'

'Is that praise? Never mind, darling, look, I got you all, but all the papers. Buriton has hit the big time.' She dumped a pile of newsprint on my table, and went upstairs. As I read I could see excited parties of students going up the hill to the campus, most of them carrying their own papers. News reports were going, as so often, to create more news. It was a heady excitement for obscure students to be able, by en-

64

joying themselves, to attract the attention of the national press, and obviously having found that they could do it, they wouldn't meekly stop. So far the articles were factual descriptions of the fire, and the death of the drugged student in it. He had, it appeared been suffocated; the fire had not reached into the room where he camped, and if he had been conscious at its start he would easily have escaped. The police had released some photographs of the young man; smiling and frank at the age of twelve and the same face transformed eight years later into a morose and suspicious mask. The police had also given out the information that arson was definitely the cause of the fire. It had started, as far as they could tell, in four places at once, and that was beyond an accident.

Reporters yesterday; today, God help me, journalists. Craftsmen, carrion crows, call us what you like. Today after years of involvement I saw my colleagues as others must, the lichen on the rock of human affairs, impudently commenting and criticising. Better an honest description from a cub reporter than the slanted picture, pushed out of true by our own personalities that such writers as myself present. I watched cars I recognised driving past my window to the university and saw familiar faces through taxi windows. They were coming to do their think pieces about our universities, the crisis of modern youth, the pressures on the next generation. Were there new insights left? Or did we write in the certainty that nobody would remember what we had told them before, that only our own cuttings albums would bear witness against us? Well, I thought, I didn't see myself writing like that again. I'd thought I could draw on a limitless capacity to be critic and audience. Today I was bankrupt.

Thea called down the stairs, 'Clovis, are you coming shopping?'

'Just a tick,' he answered. He was balancing across the arms of a chair, reading an Asterix book which was on the floor, and regularly guffawing. From time to time he read aloud some exquisitely funny pun.

When we lived in London I had tried to take Clovis out with me on Saturday mornings—to fly kites on Primrose Hill if I was free, or even to come to the television centre. In term time it was Thea's only free morning; anyway, I liked his company. He had been a solemn, polite, tiny child, with scarlet cheeks and bright eyes. He liked to wear the same coloured trousers and sweaters as I had on. When I left for the East, he was at the joke stage, punctuating his witticisms with the words, 'Get it, get it?' like a public-bar comic. He hadn't changed much while I was away. But I had. I could not, even out of politeness raise a smile any more. He asked me who had killed a quarter of the world's inhabitants, and far from remembering the correct answer—Cain—to this schoolboy chestnut, my mind sprang sickly to Hitler and Stalin, Ghengis Khan and thence eastwards. Poor Clovis.

Poor Thea too. All this was not her line. Our relationship had been one of equals. She had her own work and I had mine. We could live like friends as well as lovers; or more accurately, like lovers because we were friends. We both had diversions with other people, which we never mentioned at home, though I knew of hers and she must have known of mine. But with the front door closed on the world, our lives were flawlessly connubial.

It did not suit us now to have me dependent on Thea. But there was nothing we could do about it. She would have to look after me and I would have to submit to it, but I could sense her—not revulsion, not dislike; no, she was merely impatient. She did not like to be needed. Even her love for Clovis had always been more detached than mine. She had treated him like another person of equal status from the time he was born, respecting his needs and wishes as she was determined that he should respect hers, demanding for herself in fact a father's traditional freedom: to have his company when it suited her.

Thea does not care for her effect on my career, nor would she be more than mildly pleased to be the mother of a successful man. She has always been generous in praise, but she does not see her life in relation to ours, and she will not expect credit or blame to spread from us to her.

She came into the room carrying a muddy, twine bound cardboard box. 'I was thinking of taking up patchwork or tapestry,' she said with a wry smile.

'Company work? You needn't for my sake.'

'I've found a compromise,' she said, unwrapping the soggy parcel. 'It's all the pottery from site three at Rosewood. I shall play jigsaws with it.' She spread out some newspaper on the draining board and prepared a bowl of water to scrub the sherds. When Thea took over the department of archaeology at

Buriton she had inherited boxes of unwashed, unsorted and even unlabelled detritus of the past which had been excavated but never studied by her predecessor. Clovis helped her to lay the pieces of pottery in rows on the paper. I watched his crooked fingers moving them around at different angles. Fiddling with the brown fragments would keep Thea from total boredom when she felt obliged to sit with me. And that struck a false note too. When we lived in London there had been no question of keeping each other company. We happened to sit in the same room, or not, without reading messages of rejection into our solitude.

I said, almost involuntarily, 'Do you love me, Thea?' She raised her eyebrows, but Clovis had plugged in his radio earphone, and took no notice of us. She answered, 'Yes, of course.'

'You're disgusted by me,' I said.

'Well,' she said lightly, 'I like you better healthy than sick. But that's just as well, since you're not going to be laid up for life.' I couldn't stop myself. I said,

'Kiss me then.' She bent down and brushed her lips across my cheek, and I held her chin and pressed my mouth to hers. I pushed her away. 'You see,' I said.

'Well, I'm sorry,' she snapped. 'What do you expect me to feel? Do you suppose I like having you inaccessible in plaster casts?'

'It's not just that.'

'Oh darling, you aren't yourself—you know it as well as I do. We'll live through this, you know, we'll ride it out. But do you want me to pretend that I

68

don't like you better when you're not having a severe depression? I don't want to talk about it. Clovis, come on. We're going out.' She swept our son and herself from the room, anxious no doubt, not to say anything worse. But she didn't understand. It was her companionship she had withdrawn, the sensation of being allies. She was tolerating me.

Why couldn't Thea, I thought, be more like Jenny? I wish that my lovely girl would come and see me again. Last time she came I had spoken to her a little sharply. Was that why she had deserted me? I'd scolded her for the very qualities I loved in her. Men always destroy what they most love. She was gentle, submissive and helpful, and always believed what the person who spoke last said.

I'd met her first at a tea party Thea gave for her students, in an early effort to keep me entertained.

The young are a strange mixture nowadays, both more and less sophisticated than we were twenty years ago. Their attitude was very much that they were to be taken as found, which I thought rash. Yet they had the most practical awareness of the hard world outside the ivory tower. The difference was that they had all kept themselves financially for all the vacation months of the year. My generation sometimes had jobs as Christmas postmen, but my friends and I mostly had parents to fall back on. This lot was rationally intent on secure jobs in a labour market they already knew.

We were halfway through a stifled hour when the bell rang again. Thea's raised eyebrows showed me what a social effort she was making, and that she felt rueful about boring me. Clovis was making up a kit he had brought me hoping that I would while away some time doing it. He chose presents in the best way, giving others what he most wanted himself.

There were two latecomers; one was Jenny, ravishing with looped swags of hair around her almond smooth face and a long skirt, like one of the heroines in my current reading. She had come with Ian Macardle.

Conversation is forced on these occasions. Just as it is inevitable that dull women at parties will ask me what I do, and then tell me how fascinating it is that I do it, so one always asks students what they are reading. Jenny's voice was clear and high, sweetened by a slight Cornish burr. 'I'm reading english and archaeology,' she said. Her mouth curved upwards at the corners and her upper eyelids opened like a half moon as she smiled. One is not denatured by being encased in plaster. I shifted uneasily on my sofa, and turned my attention to the quenching young man, the very opposite of the girl in attraction, poor fellow. He looked like the stooge in a two man joke show.

'I'm doing law,' he announced. 'It's relevant, you know. Know thine enemy and what his weapons are.'

'And who is your enemy?'

'No, no,' Thea interrupted, laughing, 'don't ask him, he'll only tell you, won't you, Ian? I don't think Sylvester's strong enough.'

'I'd better not anyway, I guess,' Ian Macardle said seriously. 'Don't want you making copy out of our struggle.' A mousy young man who had been sitting cross legged and silent since he arrived, before anyone else, suddenly surprised me by speaking—or rather, by struggling to do so since he had an incapacitating stammer.

'I think it's all nonsense,' he forced out. 'All your demos, I mean. There's nothing to complain about here. They give us complete freedom. I don't know what you make all that fuss about.' He was like those stammering professional broadcasters, about whom one wonders how they got into that business in the first place, until it becomes apparent that they're worth every minute's hesitation to the producer of a thin programme. This chap went on an on, and though one could have interrupted anyone else, the endurance of such labour and hardship to speak at all earned attention. Even Ian Macardle felt obliged to listen. But he made up for it afterwards, and we were treated to a fine rehearsal of soap box oratory. It was all the usual stuff, expressed fluently but in clichés, and apart from the stammerer's ineffectual efforts to interrupt, we were all bored and stunned into silence. Even Clovis turned round and listened open mouthed, paint dripping on to his jersey as he sat with a full brush forgotten in his hand.

The frightening thing for me was that I recognised this youth: not himself, but his technique and his manners and indeed his future. He was a version of the unlikeable, self confident, conceited person who depresses us in youth and governs us in middle age. Those of my contemporaries whom he resembled were already in positions of power. I do not, it becomes apparent, much like the people by means of

71

whom I have earned fame and fortune. When, at last, he finished his peroration, I said in as patronising tone as I could manage, 'You'll go far, my boy,' but he looked gratified, not offended, and replied, in a matter-of-fact voice,

'I hope so.'

But Ian Macardle's listeners were not immediately bludgeoned into submission. The stammerer complained that it was all very well; but, he said, how could he be expected to believe in all this revolutionary egalitarianism when its chief proponent round here was the son of some aristocrat or other.

Jenny's cheeks slowly and fascinatingly blushed to the colour of her dress. She said gently,

'That's not fair. You can't know Toby, or you wouldn't bring that in. What's it got to do with anything?'

'You're just his fan, Jen, you're biased,' said the boy.

'OK, so I'm his fan. What about it? I bet you don't know Toby yourself or you wouldn't be talking like that. He's—well, different. Not like other people.'

The stammering young man spread his hands in an attempt at being funny, and looked around at the others in the room with his eyebrows raised. He'd copied the gesture, and I understood it, but it was pathetic to watch, for his acned face didn't show the emotions he felt, and his red, unlined hands protruding from too short tweed sleeves emphasised his youth. He looked like a student in a tutorial discussion with a teacher who knows all the answers, but pretends not to have heard them before. He had the opposite effect on me at least from that which he intended, giving, by his scepticism, credence to the girl. I said,

'Who is Toby, Jenny?'

'Haven't you seen him? He's impossible to describe.'

'Try,' Thea said. 'I'm fascinated.'

'Well, he's like I said, he's different. Oh, it's not just that he looks so good, there are lots of handsome men around. He doesn't get girls screaming to touch him or anything like that. But he means what he says, he gets it over, you know? Oh Ian, you explain.'

'What Jenny means is that Toby has charisma,' Ian said, but Jenny did not recognise the sarcasm and said eagerly,

'Yes, that's it. He—well, it's like one of the apostles or something, you sort of listen to him and believe what he says 'cos he's not saying it for himself, he's not going to get anything out of it, he just knows what's right and wants everything to be fair and shared out, his own things too. And when he tells you something you know it's right.'

'Amazing,' Thea commented in a mild voice. 'And what does he tell you?'

'He and I share the same views,' Ian said. And a man who had so far done nothing but eat now looked up from what must have been his tenth crumpet and said, 'Toby is the visionary and Ian the practical man, isn't that right?'

'You might put it like that, David, yes,' Ian agreed. 'I'm afraid that my feet are more firmly on the ground. Toby provides the inspiration and I do my humble best to carry it out.'

73

'Who's his father, did you say?' Thea asked.

'Duke of somewhere, but he doesn't trade on it. It's irrelevant.'

'That's all very well, Ian,' the stammerer said, 'but it means that he can fall back on rich dad. He wouldn't get much of a job with the sort of record he's got here, anyway he hasn't a hope in hell of passing the exams. What about your exams, come to that?'

'Oh that's taken care of.'

'I'll bet. But you'll have to hypnotise the examiners. I don't suppose that Toby Norman will have to work for his living, but what about you?'

Ian did not answer, but Jenny burst out,

'Honestly, you have a soul of clay.'

'Maybe, but you have to eat to live. Bread, you know what I mean?'

'Well, Toby has got enough for us all. We don't think of it as his or anything. You're bourgeois.'

Thea stood up then, looking amused. She said it was time for her to take Clovis back to school and it was a golden excuse to get our guests to leave, usually an impossible task. Once indeed some students stayed on chatting in our house in London for hours after Thea and I had gone to bed. But now they went out, probably relieved at having a duty over and at least half of them thanked Thea nicely for the tea. As Jenny murmured her goodbye to me, and hoped that I would soon be feeling better, I asked her to drop in and see me sometimes. I regretted it as soon as I spoke, and I could see that Thea was amused. But the heavenly girl smiled and agreed, and she

came as she had promised, dropping in on her way
up the hill, and delivered an azalea before Christmas
and daffodils from the Isles of Scilly for New Year.

She took her way of life for granted and would
have thought me mad to query it. She displayed a
truly liberated lack of reticence about her relationship with the young men. She worshipped Toby and
believed in him, and saw Ian as the fixer. But she
washed both their shirts, and did not speak as though
she only slept with one.

I'd asked her once if her parents didn't mind.

'Yes, my mother's very old fashioned. She hasn't
told Dad. What makes it all right for my mother is
who Toby's family are. Isn't it pathetic?' Jenny's
charity stopped at her mother, it was immediately
apparent. But I could see rather touching traces of
what Mrs Pascoe must be like in her daughter; Jenny's
manners and gestures were a give-away, and I did
not believe that she was as indifferent to Toby's background as she liked to think.

'What are Toby's family like?' I asked her.

'Oh, they're ever so nice. Terribly kind. They don't
live a bit the way you'd think. There's this enormous
house, National Trust, miles of park and all that.
You'd expect everything to be grander than—well,
than anything I'd imagined. I was terrified, actually.
But it wasn't a bit like that. They don't use the grand
bits of the place at all, when I got there with Toby
we went in at a pokey little door round the side of the
house, and they live in awfully few rooms. Fancy,
their lounge isn't as big as ours at home, and they all
sit in there, dogs, cats, Toby's mother knitting and

his father doing needlework, he's making covers for all the dining-room chairs in the part of the house they have open to the public. And there were great holes in the couch, and in the carpet. My mother would have a fit if even one of our things was like that. But they don't even seem to notice, nobody said anything about it. And it was so cold. Fancy, we've had central heating at home since I was born, but Toby's father was saying that he couldn't afford it, not even for the bit of the house they live in. They gave me a hot water bottle made out of some kind of pottery to hold on my lap.'

'Has Toby got brothers and sisters?'

'Yes, but they are all much older, and they don't live at home. His mother said he was spoilt as a child, but you wouldn't think it.' When Jenny spoke of Toby her voice softened, but she looked not so much like a girl who was in love, as like a disciple. There was something both maternal and awed about her attitude towards him. I said that I'd like to meet this hero, and she answered a little dubiously that she would bring him to see me. 'He doesn't sort of go on visits much, actually. But perhaps if I explain what a grotty time you're having ...' She had not meant to offend by making it plain that to visit me was an act of charity, and I was ashamed of my ungracious reply. Was that how I had annoyed her?

I watched idly as Thea and Clovis progressed slowly down the road. They seemed to meet a lot of acquaintances. Clovis was changing from a small boy's friendliness to a pre-adolescent gaucherie, and I saw that he was embarrassed by Thea stopping to talk to people. It shamed him to be associated in public with his parent. Yet I could not visualise him as the drug-rotted student that Winston Simpson had become; my pessimism cannot have been complete. Then I realised that Thea was talking to Esmond Smith. So the editor had given up waiting for me to report. I wasn't sure whether I minded.

Esmond came in beaming. He appears an unassertive and affectionate man, pink faced and dapper. He dips his pen in acid, however. 'My dear Sylvester.' He shook my hand for a long time. He and I joined the *Argus* at about the same time, Esmond moving from the *North Briton* in Edinburgh, and I from television. Thea thinks his wife Diana is dull and worthy. I rather like her, a plain and plump woman much involved with her house and family. But Esmond and I met more out of our homes than in them, when I lived in London.

'You've come down for the students,' I remarked.

'No no, not at all. For you, Sylvester, really. It seemed a good moment.'

'Well?' I wouldn't help him.

'You know what Bernard wants.' Bernard Trent, the editor, liked to get what he wanted. I shook my head. 'Nose to the grindstone, my dear fellow. It'll be less trouble to give in straight away.'

'I'm ill.'

'Thea tells me that your leg is doing well. And there haven't been further attacks of the other thing. Sitting still to keep clots out of your arteries doesn't involve your writing hand. Or tape the stuff, if you like.'

'Have some coffee, Esmond,' I said. 'Look, you make it. The stuff's over there.' He moved quietly around the kitchen, efficiently producing real coffee. He used to write cooking articles under a pseudonym when he lived in Scotland. I was glad to see him.

He returned to the attack later. 'You don't lose a political nose,' he insisted, 'not until you're dead. Don't tell me that you can ignore what's going on here. I know you, Sylvester, if there's nothing else within reach you'd analyse the party factions of a woman's institute.'

'Did I write to you from the East?'

'Yes. And you sent good stuff from there too. Bernard was delighted. Why?'

'Have you seen governments overthrown by students? I talked to some of the Americans out there, you know. Well meaning and generous as hell, most of them. But a few liked seeing the conditions out there. It confirmed them in what they thought about the wide world outside. Decadent and dirty, that's how they saw it. They'd watch the riots—I was with them once, behind the embassy bars—and talk about the natives as though they were monkeys. Not human at all, you know? Gooks, they called them. And then you'd look at the mob, and you'd see why, that was the awful part, those cynical yellow faces. Born older than the world, they seemed. And you'd know all the time that they were doing what they thought was the only thing left to do, that there weren't any other ways. And they didn't even know that they were being manipulated because they weren't people, they were commodities, to the others.

Bluff and double bluff and bluff cubed. I want no more part of it.'

'You have a jaundiced view,' Esmond said.

I watched a group of half a dozen students walking up the hill. Jenny was with them, beautiful, happy and innocent. The other wretches who shared the title of student with her faded from my memory as she passed the window, and I remembered all the occasions when Jenny's Toby-inspired kindness had lightened my personal darkness, even to the extent of listening to my dreams.

I couldn't tell Thea; other people's dreams bore her. And when I'd mentioned to her that I felt as though all the secrets of the universe had been revealed to me when I was unconscious, she told me that she believed it was a not uncommon illusion at such moments.

It was when I was coming round after the first anaesthetic. I've had anaesthetics before and know the slow groping towards consciousness, and the immediacy in one's mind of the moment hours before of which one was last aware. This was different, a long struggle. Objectively, it may have been a brief episode. I was an explorer in the field of humanity on behalf of extraneous observers. I was constantly being released from failed experiments, and then detailed to another artificially induced conflict, in each of which humanity failed to show any progress in goodwill or good sense. It was at the point when experiments were scrapped, with as little regard for the victims as we have for microscopic slide cultures that I was repeatedly withdrawn to realise afresh that the real world was elsewhere and humanity with its problems were unreal. I did not want to be sent back again, but felt myself receding into oblivion; and woke to the lamp-lit faces of the nursing sisters.

I know it is the disordered fancy of a delirious brain which I have inaccurately recorded here, so I cannot explain why the world still parades in my mind as though I were observing it from outside. It is not an uncommon fancy, I suppose, since it has been a popular theme for writers of science fiction ... and yet, and yet, it feels as though that were the truth and all this a dream.

Jenny was the ideal listener, with an air of sympathetic and discreet attention. I could have kissed her when she refrained from telling me that I was unbalanced, or from recommending cures. Instead she made me a pot of coffee and shared with me the lunch which Thea had left on a tray, and her presence alone was soothing.

I might have found Jenny a little irritating if I had been well. But at this time she represented sanity to me.

'Do you see that girl?' I asked Esmond.

'Which one? Oh yes. Very pretty. Delectable in fact.'

'She's called Jenny; dresses like a street Arab or like Jane Eyre, depending on her mood, and behaves like a ministering angel.'

'Thea mentioned that you were stuck into nineteenth century novels. Ministering angels don't sound quite your style, but perhaps after a course of Charlotte Yonge and the Brontes ...'

'Some of the Brontes. Not Emily. I like *Jane Eyre*, though. One hundred thousand words of wish fulfillment and the best line in fiction.'

'Really?'

'Yes—"Reader, I married him!" Irresistible. But oddly enough, Rochester in the book is described rather like Lewis Rochester here. Have you seen him?'

'No, I only know who you mean because I've read the morning papers. I didn't come down here to write about Buriton, Sylvester, but to persuade you to. Bernard has got the page's heading set up already; something about exercising your talents on politics in miniature; Sylvester Crawford sheds light on his current battle field.'

'That girl's a symbol of why I can't do it.'

'Really—'

'Her world hasn't been smirched by the likes of me, or the events I write about. I'm not even sure that all the things we write about would happen if we weren't noticing them. Like the tree in the courtyard that's only there when you look at it. I couldn't bring myself to do it.'

Thea had come into the house as I was speaking. I hoped she hadn't heard, but she said, 'You sound like a Victorian paterfamilias with ten mistresses protecting his virgin daughters' purity. I really—' She folded her lips tightly together, and turned away. Her back was eloquent.

'You might as well say it,' I told her.

'I'd better not. You're not responsible.'

'It's only my legs that were wounded, not my head.

I'm responsible.' Esmond was apparently absorbed in *Jane Eyre*, but he was too old a friend for either of us to mince our words for his sake; it was easier to make the hurtful remark with a third party there to hear it. Thea said,

'Well then, what's come over you? I know it's depressing being immobilised, I know how bored you are. I suppose it was silly to bring you down here, but I am earning a living for us.' She must really have been agitated to remind me of that, but I knew it only too well. There were natural limits to the *Argus*'s generosity. She came and sat at the table beside me, and held my hand. 'I don't feel that I'm helping you at all. If only you could occupy your mind with something. You used to be so interested in everything, it was the main thing about you. I've never known you bored before. Yet you've often stayed at home for weeks, writing something. Why is this so different? You're not in pain, after all.'

I held her hand to feel its warmth. Thea doesn't have the power of feeling with other people. She knows that it is nasty to be laid up, or to be unhappy or bored, she knows that anyone feeling such disagreeable sensations is to be pitied, but she can't imagine the actuality of it. She remembers that she has been miserable herself, but not what it felt like. I have always liked this concrete, unwhimsical outlook before, the tough and realistic quality of a person who deals in facts has happily blended with my own excessive tendency to feeling. I do not believe that to understand all is to pardon all, but I have an inconvenient leaning towards forgiveness once I have

82

made myself understand. Thea's unchanging independence from such influences was a useful prop to me when I gave way.

I said, 'Let's occupy our minds with local dramas then. What's going on today up the hill?'

'Well, lots of friends have turned up, not only Esmond. It's lovely to see you, Es,' she added, and kissed his smooth cheek as sexlessly as she kisses mine these days. 'There's Biffo,' she added, 'and Giles, and Robin, and that awful Dunster man, and even a couple of Americans. I didn't know if you'd feel like having a party?'

'What about the police? Any progress?'

'One of the students told me they were looking for bombs, but I think it was just self dramatisation. Nothing was said in the senior common room about that. There the general opinion was matches in waste paper baskets in different rooms of the house.'

'A bit chancy,' I said. 'Was anyone seen coming from it?'

'I don't think you could have noticed. There was such chaos, with the whole demo milling round before the fire was visible. But you know, what they are saying in the senior common room is that poor Winston Simpson didn't really die accidentally. It was manslaughter at the least, and murder if they just didn't bother.'

'What do you mean?'

'Well, apparently absolutely all the students knew that he was kipping there. It was a sort of standing joke against the university establishment. He used to wander round by candlelight at night and read confidential documents, and tell everyone all about them the next day. When he was *compos mentis* enough, that is.'

'You mean, that if it was a student who decided to burn the place down he simply callously ignored the fact that Simpson was probably in the house in a stupor?'

'That's what they're saying. And they all are sure it was a student. They think it was aimed at the files where applications are kept, so as to foul up the entry system for the next two years, the idea being, I suppose, that we'd then open the doors to all comers. Though I find it hard to believe that any of them would have been such nits. And as for leaving that wretched boy to suffocate or burn to death—it's not possible.'

'I must say, I'd have thought it more likely to be someone from the town than a student. At least there would be a motive—give the council a fair sickener of the university and they'll grant permission for that profit laden commercial development.'

Esmond was watching me with an amused smile, and I smiled back, slightly on the defensive. 'Just what the doctor ordered,' he said. 'An interest to take your mind off yourself. When can I tell Bernard you'll have some copy for him?'

CHAPTER FIVE

The weekend went well, in spite of the agitated parties of students and townspeople milling around Buriton. London friends, his once and future colleagues, did Sylvester a world of good. He could not stop himself from joining in their gossip, and Thea carefully refrained from letting him notice that she was aware of the difference in him. He was sufficiently perverse to lapse into depression at once if his inner eye caught sight of his own cheerfulness. The trouble was, Thea realised, that he had come home minus a sense of humour; he would find no entertainment in the picture of himself as a wounded hero at the moment, but certainly when they first came into the room, that was how his friends treated him. What, Thea crossly wondered, had he done that was so special? Sent some good reports to the *Argus* from the Far East; initiated, she had been told by Esmond Smith, a far reaching change in Foreign Office policy towards some oriental squabble; and got caught up in a riot and landed home at death's door. Many newsmen had done more than that. What about the man who told an ignorant world about the millions dying

of famine in Ethiopia? What about war corres-
pondents killed in the front line? What rendered
Sylvester's exploits interesting, she was bound to con-
clude, was that he was famous. He'd become famous
as an interviewer on television, one of the inquisitors
of the twentieth century, impaling our political
masters on skewers for us to watch. Field work was
not his line, and it was the fact that he had done it
at all that impressed everyone. Moving from the small
screen to the pages of the *Argus* was all right; a step
sideways and good for highbrow prestige, perhaps even
a stepping stone to a constituency for himself. But he
was not cut out to be a man of action, and eighteen
months' sight of horrors he had spent a lifetime
calmly describing at second hand had worked a
disastrous change in his personality.

Thea was worried, in fact, and was masking the
worry by her spiteful meditation. Naturally any wife
would worry about a husband who is delivered home
on a stretcher after several weeks in Graham Greene-
land. But she had not expected him to be quite so
gloomy. He was on the mend by now. The badly set
fracture had been rebroken and reset in an American
hospital, and though he was to be encased in plaster
for weeks she could really not think why this should
affect his personality. She had known about words like
post-operative depression, but when she came into
contact with somebody who was suffering from it,
the temptation to say 'snap out of it' was hard to
resist.

It became a guilty pleasure to leave the house in
the morning. She went out at the back of the house,

through one of the pedestrian alleys which criss-crossed around Buriton and made the town so agree-able to live in, and across a sweetly scented garden on the other side of which a stable had been con-verted into a row of garages. Then she would drive the long way round so as to go past the window where Sylvester lay. How rarely she saw him reading or writing; how frequently he lay unconstructive and miserable, reminding her each time that a better wife would be staying at home to nurse him. His unhappiness became Thea's burden, but she could shed most of its weight as she drew further from the source. She was too clear-headed to pretend that she was working to support the family; archaeology was a luxurious self indulgence; no twists of the academic conscience could persuade her that the world would be a less happy place if her work were left undone. Even to ninety per cent of the students it would be a matter of indifference whether they were learning archaeology or astronomy or even astrology; the subject's lectures had merely happened to fit into vacancies on their timetables at the beginning of the year.

It was a perpetual subject for argument among the staff of the university, whether they should complain about or report the students who made too obvious their lack of interest in the subjects they were supposed to be studying. The university was now officially run as an equal partnership between staff and students; to send down an unsatisfactory student had been unusual and now would not happen at all. There was simply no sanction if somebody chose not to turn up to classes or write essays. To threaten with examination failure seemed petty when one believed that a subject was worth studying in itself and not as a passport to later employment.

The problem replaced the one of her husband in Thea's mind on this day because she had been wondering what to do about Jenny Pascoe. Why did they send these girls to universities? Oh, she thought, one knew why: if they could scrape up good enough exam results they added to the glory of their school. There was a great pressure on girls, and on boys, to lengthen the number of university successes in the speech day programme. That was the criterion by which schools were judged these days.

But Jenny Pascoe, who had apparently completely given up any pretence of attendance at classes, could not, by Thea, be treated like any other student. One could not allow oneself to be thought jealous. Thea was in any case only too pleased that some of Sylvester's dismal and idle hours should be entertained by such a pretty poppet; indeed, she was almost sorry that he could not do anything but talk and look at her— something more would be such a morale booster.

Thea's mouth twisted a little wryly as she remembered some of the girls who had diverted Sylvester in the past years. It would have been unreasonable to make scenes when he fell for such delicious bait. But he was the one who started it. Thea had married with every intention of fidelity. It had taken all her intellect, all her powers of reason, to rise above the knowledge of his first girl friend, a production assistant à la Bardot. Sylvester was of the generation to whom hair like a haystack and a mouth like a cushion represented the acme of sexiness. I wasn't playing tit-for-tat, she thought, thinking of her own extra-marital career; it wasn't to get my own back on him. But there had not seemed much point in observing customs that he ignored, and Thea had soon come to realise that they were obsolete for people like herself. She enjoyed her adventures, and they had never touched her emotions. But she still thought that she would have been chaste if he had.

Thea was the daughter of a Manchester doctor. Proximity to much poverty, a school which aimed at Oxbridge or nowhere, and an environment which —incredible as it seemed in retrospect—allowed her to reach the age of twenty-one without ever having heard of masturbation or Lesbianism, had turned Thea into something of an intellectual prig. She read no novels and never speculated about other peoples' emotions. But she was more dependent on Sylvester than he realised. He had always needed the freedom that knowing she was free gave him, and she had not doubted the importance of her own professional life. But it had been a struggle for her to accept what he was sure of, that her work was as important as his. And having learnt a lesson from him which most wives fail in a lifetime to teach their husbands, Thea still found herself bound by self-imposed restrictions. She had sexual freedom years before she was able to regard her own image as more than an appendage of Sylvester's. She wore bonds that he had never wished to forge. For the last few years in London Thea had subconsciously forced herself to behave like a traditional wife, frantically cooking and home-making when she came in from work to prove to some invisible censors that she fulfilled her proper role. It was not Sylvester who held her back, and yet it had been a gesture of defiance on Thea's part to apply for the job at Buriton when Sylvester went abroad, and as it were unilaterally to shift the family home. Over those years she attributed to him motives he never had, and had liberated herself with an effort from a non-existent restraint.

But Thea enjoyed the new life, however illusory the sensation of liberation, and she realised herself that it was unfair to grudge Sylvester his place in it, as she did. She was too busy for the gentling and jollying he needed; therefore, Thea thought, it was just as well that he had found Jenny to do the feminine bit.

Thea wondered whether it was Sylvester's sophisti-cated influence which had changed the girl. She used to appear in garments which would, ten years before, have provoked that immortal comment, *Tiens, on dirait un bal masqué*. But recently Jenny had taken to wearing positively adult clothes, really far more so than Thea, still clinging to the licence offered to the middle aged by possession of a good figure and flowing hair, would herself be seen in. Jenny still looked a little fancy-dressed. A black crepe dress with pearls was, after all, unsuitable both for the univer-sity campus, and for somebody not yet nineteen.

Thea pulled her thoughts up. She had not been aware of feeling any jealousy of the girl, certainly not in regard to Sylvester, so why this definitely catty turn to her thoughts? There was no reason to dislike her. It was a case of 'Mirror mirror on the wall'. Thea was pretty, and had been referred to as a girl for more years than most women. It was only when one saw, or was seen with, girls like Jenny that the unintentional pretence became precious. Thea had always admitted to her age, because she knew she did not look it. Jenny Pascoe made her feel it.

All the more reason, perhaps, to take a little extra bit of trouble over the girl. Thea had looked up the address, and decided that she would go over to the house and see what had become of Jenny Pascoe. Perhaps she was sulking after her experience in police cells.

The street she found was an Edwardian row of villas, near but not in sight of the sea, built at the time when boarding houses flourished and Buriton was successful as a family resort, livelier than Frinton or Penzance, more genteel than Brighton or Newquay. The street reminded Thea of biographies, in which sad old men poured out on to the page their obsessions about childhood and nanny and halcyon days before the prison of prep-school. This sunlit street was peopled with the ghosts of well fed children carrying buckets and spades and shrimping nets, blinking into the stained glass hall to sniff the landlady's Irish stew and blancmange and boast about donkey rides and Punch and Judy shows.

Jenny's house stood out from the rest, as it was almost the only one in the street which did not have a painted name, like Shalimar, or Dunroamin, or Pontefract, above a neat 'Bed and Breakfast' sign.

It looked downcast and shabby, and the front garden had been paved over to make a car space, on which stood a slogan painted, fluorescent mini-van.

The front door was open on to a long passage. The old wrought iron umbrella stand was still there, containing a brass musical instrument and a shepherd's crook. The bell did not work, and Thea rapped her knuckles against a fire-engine bell which hung without its clapper from the fretwork porch. A voice called,

'Come in—I'm here.' Thea stepped into the house, feeling that her heels sounded alien and middle aged on the tiled floor. The first room she looked into was bare boarded, and contained nothing but two uncovered duvets, and a pottery mug full of Indian incense sticks, but the sickly-sweetish smell was actually cannabis.

Jenny Pascoe was in the back room, stirring something on what passed for a stove—a couple of bottled-gas rings mounted on an orange box.

'Oh hullo,' she said, not sounding very surprised. 'Sorry—I can't stop till it's thickened.'

'What are you making? It smells lovely.'

'There's a kidney casserole in the hay box: *à la madère*, you know. And this is going to be *zabaglione*.'

'Goodness, how elaborate. Do you always cook such lavish food, or are you having a party? I'm sorry to interrupt you.'

'No, we've lived on whole food and health food for ages now. Macrobiotics, yin and yan, you know. But I suddenly felt like something else. I got a steak last night, but the others wouldn't eat it. They probably won't even have this pudding, it's made with wine, but that's too bad. I think it's about time we grew up a bit.'

Thea looked round the room while Jenny pouted over her saucepan. There was a miscellaneous collection of improbable furniture, some of it made with foam rubber, brick and planks, but other pieces which must have come as cast offs from Toby's home, a marble topped, semi circular table on an elaborate gilt base, a tall mahogany corner cupboard and a velvet chaise longue, among other things. There were the usual posters of the younger generation's heroes, and a large scale map of the district pasted on the wall, as well as an oil painting which looked like a Landseer —a panting spaniel and majestic stag—and an extremely large photograph in sepia of a woman closely resembling Queen Alexandra. In one corner was a pile of dresses and materials. Some of them had been cut up, and there were some paper hexagons spilling out of a bag, ready stitched for patchwork.

Jenny was dressed in an extremely neat trouser suit with the sleeves pushed back to show gold bangles, which matched her small earrings. She had on a lot of make-up, skilfully applied, and smelt of a good scent. Thea wondered if all this was for Sylvester. She said, 'It's so good of you to go and cheer up my husband.'

'Oh, I like it, he's very sweet,' Jenny said, absent-minded. She held up the spoon and watched the viscous drops sliding down it. 'I'd say that was done, wouldn't you?'

'Yes. It'll curdle if you go on.'

'That's what I thought.' She took three pottery bowls off a shelf and poured equal quantities into each. 'I must get some glass dishes,' she muttered, and unselfconsciously licked the spoon. Her attention was fully on the work in hand, and Thea braced herself, to talk as moral tutor to a girl *in statu pupillari*. Thea was leaning against a stack of shelves, made of planks laid across concrete blocks. She turned to see what books there were, an automatic reaction to any bookshelf; all the usual revolutionary literature, of course, as well as two sets of Tolkien's complete works, *Jonathan Livingstone Seagull, Watership Down*, and various other twentieth century cult volumes. Thea had heard of all but read none. She pulled a book about self sufficient living out; some pamphlets came from the shelf with them, and she paused in the act of pushing them back; typed, duplicated, stencilled across with the red warning *'Care! Secret! Our life in your hands!'*; what were they, she wondered, idly. The words were set out in the form of an instruction pamphlet, as it might be about home electrical repairs or dressmaking. But the ingredients were wire, nails, petrol, and even gelignite: she was holding instructions distributed by an Irish undercover organisation to 'Freedom Fighters' where ever they were.

Jenny had her back to Thea, and was washing out her saucepan with a slimy rag. Thea stuffed the bundle of paper into her large shoulder bag, and when the door opened, she was leafing through *The Morte d'Arthur*.

The two young men came into the room. Jenny

94

said, without turning round, 'Hullo, had a good morning?'

'Yeah—but where were you?' said Ian.

'We missed you,' Toby said in a gentle voice, and he smiled at Thea. 'Hullo.'

'This is Professor Crawford, Toby,' said Jenny. 'You know.'

'Yes, good.' He looked friendly, but since he had nothing else that needed saying, said nothing, but sat down at the table looking benevolent.

'We don't drink here,' said Ian. 'Would you like some fruit juice?'

'Oh, I've got some sherry,' Jenny interrupted.

'Sherry? We don't drink alcohol—what did you go and get that for? Toby—did you hear? Jenny's bought some sherry.'

'Did you?' Toby asked her. His voice held no accusation or surprise, but she answered defensively, 'Well, I thought I would. It's an acquired taste, like olives. One's got to learn.'

'I suppose so—if you feel the need,' he said a little sadly. 'It affects one's responses, I'm afraid. Look, Jenny, my shoe has come apart.' He held out a dirty canvas shoe to her, and she took it automatically.

'How on earth did you do that? Oh, never mind, I can mend it. Pass me the sewing box, Ian, will you?' Ian brought the box to her, and stood with his hand on the side of her neck kneading it gently. She pushed his hand away, and said,

'Later. I'm busy.'

Thea stood up. She said,

'Well, I only came to see what had happened to you.

95

Jenny. You haven't been seen at the university for some time.'

'I didn't know. Where've you been, Jenny?' Ian said.

'Somebody's got to do the housekeeping round here,' she said.

'But we've always done it together—what do you mean? You haven't been cooking that sort of food again, have you?' He looked at the pile of dishes on the chipped enamel surface. 'You've bought meat again, I can smell it. For heaven's sake girl, what's come over you? Meat and alcohol—and look at your clothes! Toby, do you see what Jenny's up to?'

Toby Norman got up and put his arm around Jenny. She did not push him away as she had Ian, but his embrace looked brotherly.

'Do you want to change the way we live?' he said.

'Well, we are growing up. One can't pretend for ever.'

'Pretend?'

'Oh, you know. Play at houses and all that. After all, there's a big wide world outside.'

Thea did not think that this theory sounded as though Jenny had invented it; nor apparently did Toby, for he put Jenny gently at arm's length, with his hands on her shoulders, and gazed into her face. She shrugged impatiently, and said,

'What must you think of us, Professor? Do have some of the famous sherry anyway.' But Thea refused, and left rather hastily, for she felt very much like an intruder on this unusual family life.

It was brilliant weather and the whole town was

sparkling. She decided to do some errands in the town, to put off facing the worry and recriminations by which the campus would certainly be gripped. She felt a restless need for the type of action she had not taken for years—to run, or shout, or dance. She diagnosed her need more precisely as she walked: she wanted to have an affair—not of the heart, for life was already sufficiently complicated, but a simple fling with—ah, there was the rub; with whom? Lewis Rochester had a certain overbearing attraction. He would be nice, she thought, to sleep with but not to kiss. But she had seen him gawping at the girl students. He was out. There was too much difference between herself these days and for instance, Jenny Pascoe. She was, at the age of thirty-eight, thinking *si jeunesse savait, si vieillesse pouvait,* when she was greeted by Desmond Pascoe. Not, in fact, she realised, an impossible coincidence, since her stroll along Fore Street had taken her to the shop in which the exhibition was going on; and she smiled at the thought which sprang to her mind. He would definitely not 'do'.

As they stood politely chatting, a middle aged woman came up to them and thrust forward a long sheet of paper.

'It's a petition, Mr Pascoe,' she said. 'Do sign, both of you, please.'

'What is it?' Thea asked.

'About the students. We've got to do something about it. They are ruining our town. My husband had three cancellations for the hotel this very morning. After all, if people come here on holiday it's peace and quiet they want, isn't it?'

'This is Professor Crawford, from the university,' Desmond Pascoe said gently. 'I think perhaps—not this morning . . .'

'Oh. Well, I'm sorry. I suppose you're not responsible. But somebody is. We're not going to stand for it, I can tell you. Who pays the rates here anyway? I'll wish you good morning, Mr Pascoe.' She stumped angrily off, but looking around Thea could see that she was not alone in her protest. There were several people holding clipboards with papers, and they seemed to be finding no difficulty in getting people to sign. A group of young people went by who may not even have been students, but they were wearing denim and sheepskin, and attracted resentful glances. One choleric looking old man went past with a basket of food hooked on his arm and library books slipping out from under it, and he kept turning awkwardly around to look at them; Thea watched him spitting ostentatiously into the gutter.

'How they are disliked,' she said to Desmond Pascoe.

'I'm afraid so. But they don't much care.'

'Is it just the demos?'

'Not entirely. But you know, in a town like Buriton, we have a lot of pensioners, old retired people on small incomes, and then a good many of our own young people are unemployed. We've hardly any industry, except tourism. You can't really wonder that they resent the students. Grants may be small, but they still come out of the pockets of the rest of us?'

'Is that how you feel yourself then?'

'No, I don't. You may be surprised—a local councillor like me, in business in the town, you'd expect me to think they are all a crowd of layabouts. But I'm all in favour of education. I'm constantly realising what I missed myself. That's why I was so keen for my Jenny to go. Actually, I've been associated with the Rochesters for years.'

Thea had hardly had anything to do with the town since she moved to the university of Buriton. One of her friends was married to a solicitor there, and she had met a few people at her house, but there seemed to be a great divide. The staff of the university lived on, but not in Buriton. No wonder, in that case, that the citizens disliked it.

'Come and see the exhibition,' Desmond Pascoe suggested. He put his hand through her arm, and drew her towards the shop, which had 'to let' notices above it, but whose windows were filled with posters inviting people to come in and see scale models of the developments proposed for Buriton. Inside were two tables; on one was the model of the office and shop complex of buildings proposed for Freeman's Common by the company which Desmond Pascoe represented. Prominently arrowed was the day centre for old people. There was a big profit to be made there. On the other table the university's architects had displayed a miniature of a tower designed to house the whole, much expanded social science faculty. The plan had provoked much internal controversy in the senate chamber and the students' union. Its perpetrators were variously described as

99

visionaries or vandals, and its supporters as reactionaries or iconoclasts. It was this scheme, in fact, now several years old, which had impelled the students to their now historic struggle to gain representation on the senate. It was hard to understand why the issue had aroused such strong feelings in them. With a three year span as a student, none of those there now would see even the foundations dug. And the council in whose hands the decision lay, before the ritual series of appeals and counter appeals to inspectors from Whitehall and ministers, moved more slowly than the mills of God.

'Whose is Freeman's Common now, actually?' Thea asked Desmond Pascoe.

'It was given to the town two hundred years ago,' he told her, 'but the former town council went to the Chancery court about it and it turned out that they could sell the land. That was years ago, of course; your university has been negotiating for a long time. My scheme is a very late comer. But you see, it's the only land left to build on in the place, unless we take your playing fields.'

'There must be a lot of money in this.'

'I won't deny it. But it's up to the council to decide who to sell the common to; we've both applied for outline planning permission. And of course I withdraw from meetings whenever it's mentioned. I must wait as patiently as you.'

'You have a strong ally, Mr Pascoe.' A man in a dark suit who had been standing on the other side of the room came over, and shook Desmond's hand.

'Have I? This is Mr Elwood, the town clerk,' he

added, and Thea shook hands with him, wondering whether she had ever met a town clerk before, or whether she knew what they did. He opened out the local paper he was holding, and spread it on top of the tiny plastic trees which decorated the model. He pointed to the leading article, which was presumably a well timed attempt to influence events. Why, it asked, should the ratepayers of Buriton deprive themselves of a benefit for the sake of a university? What good did it do, nowadays? Times had changed since the nineteenth century university of Buriton was a highspot in Cornish life. The modern students disrupted traffic with their marches, and tempers with their arrogance; they did not bring much money into the town, they had made themselves unpopular. The elected representatives of the people should vote where their inclination and duty both lay when the question of Freeman's Common came up before the council.

'Will that help?' Thea asked.

'So so.' Mr Pascoe made a see-saw gesture with his hand. 'I don't think one can predict the outcome. The university isn't popular, it's true, but the old stagers still think of it with some pride. And big business isn't entirely beloved, as you perhaps know.'

Thea realised that the morning had brought home to her something she had not fully accepted before, that subconsciously she, like Sylvester, was only lodging in Buriton. Her mind's eye did not show her own figure in the future Buriton, as she pictured the alternative buildings there. When she came, she had long term plans for the work she would do and what she would achieve. Now her emotions, before being instructed to do so by her brain, were planning the next move.

She examined the scale models, and would have found it difficult to choose which should be built. She would not be there to see.

Most of the people in the room were considerably more involved. A large number of citizens had come in to view the alternatives, and from their loud, uninhibited remarks made clear where they stood. Desmond Pascoe seemed to know nearly everybody. He greeted men and women alike with handshakes and personal enquiries. The latest student 'outrage' was being discussed. It was enlightening to hear it from the other side.

The general opinion was that the students had had it their own way for too long. A very articulate woman was explaining that the student bodies had exploited their privileged position and run rings around all authority. If arrested for a criminal offence, they were let off lightly on the grounds that they were students, although it was for that very reason that they were in the dock in the first place; judges would be lenient to them, saying that their lives were before them and all that, while on the same day they would send working youngsters down with indelible stains on their records. Or if the university took the rare course of administering internal discipline, it was thought unfair to punish twice for the same offence. Nor would the university send them down if they were punished by some miniscule fine, for the same reason. So the end result, the woman insisted, was that they could get away scot free and laugh at the law which other people must obey. It shouldn't be allowed.

Thea was surprised at the agreement this speech evoked. After all, Desmond Pascoe could not be the only person listening whose own child was a student.

'What about your Jenny then, Mr Pascoe?' The angry woman asked. 'I saw her marching with those other kids the other day. I don't know how you can bear to let her—'

'Jenny doesn't live at home any more,' he said.

'One of those dreadful halls of residence, I suppose.'

'No, she lives in a flat with some friends. Girls, naturally. She really works very hard, doesn't she, Professor Crawford?'

'Oh—yes. Yes, certainly,' Thea lied. All eyes in the room were turned upon her. She felt, as a representative of that unpopular establishment, the university, like a visitor from Mars, and wondered how it was possible that there should be such a gulf between the town and the gown. After all, there were evening classes, surely, and lunch time concerts and —she racked her brains—yes, the university theatre. There was some common ground.

'Well, I think it's about time we organised ourselves,' the woman insisted. 'Make sure that they pay the penalty this time. After all, there's been murder done.'

'No, not murder,' Desmond Pascoe protested.

'Oh, split legal hairs if you like, that's a man all over. I call it murder, and I don't doubt that the

103

poor boy's mother does too. Wanton, senseless destruction. They deserve to go down for years.'

'Why do you dislike the students so much?' Thea asked.

'Why don't I like them? What a question! Still, I suppose you wouldn't know, if you're a teacher up there yourself. Funny job for a woman, being a professor, isn't it?' In a typically English way, most of the other people in the room were not appearing to listen. Those who had not already slipped out of the door were examining the models with intense concentration; 'I'll tell you why we've had enough of them, if you want to know. We're sick of seeing the long-haired layabouts cluttering up our town. They're killing the tourist trade, and we don't get other industry here because the government won't let us. And who pays for them, that's the real point? I'll tell you, we do. The tax payer. We keep them in idle luxury, and how do they repay it? I wouldn't mind if they were a bit grateful, if they showed they appreciated what they were getting. Nobody stood me three years to do nothing when I was young. I don't mind the ones like Mr Pascoe's Jenny. He pays for her, that's up to him. Though I hear you're in trouble, Mr Pascoe, someone said that if you didn't get this contract your shareholders—but I'd better not—anyway, like I said, it's all right if their fathers pay for them. But the rest should do a job of work. That's what I say.'

Desmond Pascoe was obviously embarrassed, and he managed to steer Thea from the room. 'I wonder what you think of Buriton after that,' he said.

'Don't worry about it. I was actually just realising how little I know of the place, to tell you the truth.'

'You haven't been getting around much?'

'I'm afraid not,' Thea said. 'Well, you know how it is. I've had a lot to do ...'

'It would give me great pleasure to show you round one day,' he said. 'I've lived here all my life, my family's been in this part of the world for centuries. Just working people, you know. My father was a fisherman. I can remember the days when the fishing fleet went out—you'd hardly believe it now—the numbers of vessels there were. It was a hard life, but a fair one, if you know what I mean. Fighting the elements and not government regulations.'

'But you didn't follow in your father's foot-steps?'

'No future in it. The trade was dying even when I was a boy. But you ought to see a bit of the Buriton we natives live in. I daresay you've looked at the show places—the tourist draws—'

'There are some lovely buildings here. Even the old university buildings—'

'Yes, it's a pity they ever moved up the hill. But I don't mean just the bricks and mortar. You don't get the feel of a place gawping from the outside. And after all, you are living here.' He guided her off the crowded pavement, through an arched opening under one of the Georgian houses. On either side were modern shops, with gangways of bright goods visible through their plate glass windows, which had been inserted into the ground floor of the old houses. The only unspoilt building in Fore Street was the pillared

Customs House, with freshly painted Royal Arms above its entrance. But through the alley where Desmond Pascoe was now leading the way, was a glimpse of the old Buriton: the same blue sea, the same striated cliffs at the far arms of the bay were visible to modern as to long dead eyes. The lighthouse was nineteenth century, and the perfect dome of the observatory had been built between the world wars. Desmond said,

'My ancestors wouldn't recognise this Buriton. It was just a small fishing village with the most fertile land in the west country around it.'

'All built over now, of course.'

'It's what people like you call bungaloid growth, isn't it? I like it myself. Some of the estate roads are called after the old fields they were put on, and my back garden grows the best nectarines in Cornwall. But otherwise it's all changed, right round the bay. It's a big town now.'

'And you were responsible for a lot of it,' Thea said.

'A certain amount, yes. I'm proud of what I've built, too. I love this place. I'm going to leave it better than I found it.'

'A good non-conformist ambition.'

'I'm the product of my environment,' he said. Thea had not expected such detachment from him. They walked to the edge of the quay where fishing boats were tied up to iron bollards and launches awaited their cargoes of tourists for the trip round the bay. The water was still with grease and scum on the surface. Oil tankers sailed by on the horizon. Rows of yachts and cruisers floated in the bay, masts bare like pea sticks; a few early dinghy sailors were taking advantage of the good weather. Desmond Pascoe pointed eastwards towards the hideous chimneys of the power station.

'I bet you hate the sight of that.'

'Don't you?'

'Ah, there's the difference between you university people, and me. You like the cottages that haven't any plumbing, the old houses in the town that even the university found unworkable and moved away from. I'm the one that loves this place, but I'm a realist. I want it to go on being a living town, not a quaint museum for tourists and incomers. I like the power station because it represents what we need. Industry, full employment, independence of begging. Look'— he held out his hands with the curled fingers upwards in the classic mendicant gesture. 'Look at my starving child, pity my infirmities and give. It's only different in degree from begging for money in exchange for a sight of the decrepit houses and the useless fishing boats. These boats don't go out for pilchards or mackerel, you know. They take the summer visitors shark fishing. We get our fish from Grimsby.'

'You speak about tourists rather like that lady spoke about students, don't you?'

'Both parasites, you mean? Don't you think it's a point of view?'

'But not yours?'

'No, I told you, I'm all for education. Many an argument I've had with my wife about that. But I was determined that my Jenny should have what I missed.'

'Didn't your wife want her to?'

'No, she was all set on her being a secretary, or a nursery school teacher. Something she called more feminine.' Thea smiled at him, and jumped herself up to sit on the granite balustrade. The spring sun was warm on her back. It felt agreeably irresponsible to sit and chat about abstracts on what should be a working day.

'I'd have expected you to be keen on the feminine pursuits,' she said.

'Really? No, I like high powered women. I'd like to see Jenny having a proper career, do something in the world. And be a wife and mother too, of course. But she needs more to be interested in than her— than most women.'

Thea felt sorry for the man. He had apparently grown away from a conventional wife, and would, in Thea's view, be disappointed by a daughter destined for the most unremarkable life. But he could hardly have educated his child to model her behaviour on that of his mistress.

'Has your wife a career?' Thea asked, with a quirk of malice.

'No, she's very occupied with domestic interests, and her charities, the bridge club—you know the kind of thing.' He looked at her with amusement. 'You're mincing your words, aren't you?'

'Well, I could hardly—'

'No; but we're both thinking of the same thing. After all, you're not one of my moral judges. Not that this town isn't full of them. But you are not part of it, are you? I don't see you staying here long.'

'I have no plans for moving.'

'Unlike someone else we know. But then you're happily married—more's the pity!' His eyebrows were comically raised, his glance worldly. Thea thought, I like this man very much. Joyce Rochester and I have similar tastes. She said,

'I gather divorce is still frowned on down here.'

'Yes, our friend's plans to move are well timed.'

'And are you moving away too?'

'I suppose I asked for that,' he said, laughing. 'No, this is my place, I stay put at Lamorna Villa, unless I go bankrupt or something. And our mutual friend is probably as anxious as I am that it shouldn't happen. But I couldn't leave my wife, you know. She hasn't anyone else.'

'I wasn't suggesting—' Thea protested.

'Yes you were! And I don't blame you. No, Joyce and I will carry on as we were. It's not as though we want more children, after all. You don't understand us yet, we all go by appearances here. You are not the right sort of person for this life. You are what you seem, and very nice too.' Thea jumped down from the wall and brushed grit from the seat of her skirt. They walked along the quay side. 'Now Rochester,' he said. 'There's an example for you of someone who flies the right flags.'

'He appears to conform, you mean? Is it so difficult?'

'Not for him. He acts the way an occasion calls for, but it comes naturally to him. Do you know what I mean? He'd bow to royalty one minute and sit cross legged at a guru's feet the next without turning a hair. Performing comes naturally to him.'

'Lucky him,' Thea said.

'I suppose so. But I sometimes wonder who is there when he is alone in a room.'

'One can see what you feel about him.'

'No, you're wrong.' Desmond Pascoe stopped and put his hand on Thea's arm. His grasp was warm and firm; he had long square fingers with hair around the knuckles. 'I don't dislike the man, we're too alike, with him running his universities, and me doing my public work in Buriton. He's a powerful character, and I may not understand him, but I do admire him. He gets things going. Oh, he may be a bit of a cold fish—though perhaps you find him attractive. My information may have been biased.'

'He can certainly make himself attractive if he wants to,' Thea said.

'There you are. He turns it on if there's a good reason. But who is to say that he's wrong to use all the weapons he's got? I use mine—knowing who people are, their weaknesses and prejudices, just knowing who their grandfathers were. That's the way of local politics. No, we're both Mr Fixits.'

'My husband thinks Lewis Rochester is very ambitious. Are you?'

'In my fashion. But my sphere is a local one. You'll read about me in the *Buriton Packet*. Rochester gets into *The Times*.' They had walked to the bottom of the street which led up to the university. Thea stopped and looked up at Desmond Pascoe.

'You've spoken very freely to me,' she said.

'One can, to an outsider. And apart from that ...'
They smiled at one another, implicitly accepting and
regretting that in other circumstances they could have
gone further together. 'I'd like my Jenny to model
herself on you. She's lucky to have you as a teacher.'

'I'm afraid I'm not the one Jenny's modelling herself on,' Thea said drily. 'You'll have to look elsewhere for the person who is an influence on her.'
They shook hands and parted. Desmond Pascoe was
instantly accosted by one of his electors, and Thea
walked home to Sylvester.

CHAPTER SIX

Did I care whodunnit? What was the death of one junkie to me, or the destruction of one building? What would it be to anyone in a hundred years?

But the habit of years dies hard. I couldn't help wondering about the events in Buriton, though I meanly tried not to give Thea the satisfaction of knowing I was interested when she told me about them. The methods of police investigation were easy enough to guess, and the group of people on whom they concentrated. I was not surprised, though the student body was astonished, when, in the middle of the next week, Ian Macardle was arrested and charged with arson. Another charge was to follow, and it was not hard to work out that it would be of manslaughter at the least, perhaps even murder. He was remanded in custody after a brief hearing at the magistrates' court at which he reserved his defence.

This correct legal procedure, I hardly need add, provoked astonished outrage in the student world. It also had the incidental effect of relieving Thea.

I had noticed her uneasiness. For several days it was apparent that there was something she was being careful not to mention to me. It was only after Ian's arrest that she told me about the pamphlet that she had found at his house, and that she had passed it on to the police. She had undergone an acute crisis of conscience, not knowing whether unworthy malice or commendable public spirit persuaded her to do so. But she didn't like Jenny, she told me rather defiantly, and she was afraid that she would be indulging her own irrational likes and dislikes if she exposed her to police investigation. And she feared that I would become agitated in my reproaches to her. I don't know whether she was right to fear it, but in the event it appeared that only Ian had been seen near the back entrance of the registry building, at a time when Toby and Jenny were already on their way to the cells in police cars after obstructing the fire engines. Ian had been seen by no less a person than the principal himself.

Invariably, inevitably, Ian was described, in their polysyllabic jargon, as a public martyr of authoritarian victimisation. It had been thought and hoped that a student charged with a crime of this nature— on another level, after all, from the usual conspiracy and obstruction charges—could not become a hero of the grassroots. Murder isn't a matter of degree, after all.

But the optimism of the adults was dashed by an immediate, almost Pavlovian reaction. From my window I watched the gathering crowds over the next days. Undeterred by the laws about contempt of court, or matters which are sub judice, the young politicians were gathering their forces for protest and demonstration. Initially nothing more than a show of solidarity was projected, but this merged into strength and thence into pressure. After a week of speeches outside my window and duplicated sheets of instruction and encouragement, I realised that when Ian Macardle came to trial, his colleagues would be trying to influence the process of the law. Would Rochester dare to give evidence against Ian with thousands of students waiting outside the court room to blame him? Would he have the courage, knowing that his own students preferred passive resistance, to provoke mass riots and disobedience from members of other universities? And yet they were clever enough not to spell out this dilemma; the threat was tacit and one could not accuse anyone in particular of making it.

The date of the trial had been fixed for the end of March. There were some students left in the university who wanted to get on with their academic work and Thea and the other members of the staff continued with their teaching programme as the timetable dictated.

I was once in a country where there was an ultimatum of war, deferred for four weeks. I was only an outsider with a duty to note the anguish and terror of others as though it were nothing to do with me. Nor it was, in fact: they laid on special planes for foreigners before the action began. During those weeks it took an intellectual effort to realise from the outside what was in store. One looked at the streets of shoppers and children living an ordinary life. It was a country of gregarious people and the groups of chatting citizens at street corners might have featured in a tourist brochure. But indefinable, almost palpable, was the foreboding. They were numbering their days.

So, in Buriton, the volcano was signalling eruption. At least that was how the students liked to see it. They went about the business of studying with an air of slyness, of glee. Balloons coming out of their heads would have read *Little do they know!* I was sorry for them. One could envy the security of an environment which made student protest into a major event; how enviable to have no more desperate preoccupation. But how ludicrous, all the same, to take that, of all things, seriously.

In myself, as the term went on, I improved. I was actually thinking about things and people as though they were interesting. I began to see the view from the window, instead of the jaundiced distortion of it which my illness had projected.

It had been a mild winter in Buriton, at least since my arrival there shortly after Christmas. I had been told about Cornish gales and the occasional snow thick enough to close main roads and even railways, but the local people are always taken by surprise and Clovis complained that none of the shops stocked toboggans. He had not needed one yet, for it had been raw and damp and dismal but the thermometer kept above the mid-forties and the barometer stayed low.

There should be a calm pleasure in following the progress of the ships in the bay, the rise and fall of the signal above the observatory, the regular flashes and moans of the lighthouse, and there should be a disinterested observer's satisfaction in charting the movements of our neighbours, and watching the progress of the common from mud patches to snow-drop drifts. Crocuses came early, with the visible promise of daffodils and tulips to come. This morning a kind neighbour had brought me a vase of citrus scented magnolias.

It was, as often, raining that fine western precipitation which one can hardly see, and whose existence I could only confirm by looking at the puddles on the road. I watched children skipping in brightly coloured mackintoshes, splashing their gumboots in the water. I watched the local ladies walking down the hill with empty baskets and scampering dogs, and returning with heavy loads and weary companions. I watched old gentlemen come home with their papers under their arms, or with piles of books from the library: lovable, real, respectable people. But my heart, fluctuating like a yo-yo, was heavy.

I had seen little of Jenny, and when she came it was with manners overlaying grace. Some of the time I did not care. I would look at the other girls who went past my house, all ardent young animals, and wonder whether they were distinguishable? Was there anything unique about Jenny that she would not be interchangeable with her contemporaries? Or about me, or Thea, or Clovis? Even I had sometimes failed to recognise him, my only son, when he was with a group of boys all in uniform (jeans: he'd been at a progressive school in London). Would it matter to the world to be one boy in millions the less? It was the same old argument as about abortion; how many Beethovens, or Hitlers, have we lost?

I think, for instance of my sister, who makes friends and leaves them behind when she moves house every two years, shifting from one identical married quarter to the next. The army wives she meets must be so much of a kind that it hardly matters whether she's talking to Shirley or Jane or Penny. Any woman of the right age, conforming to the twentieth century western average, would do to talk about nursery schools and washing machines with; their talk is the Muzak of conversation.

But I must be returning to my old self; I found my emotions revolting against the idea that Clovis was of no more importance than any other two legged animal. I'd relearnt the value of the individual.

So my spirits lifted when Jenny appeared, though dashed again by the sight of her companion. She introduced her as her mother. I could see the likeness. This woman had once been a very pretty girl, but was now only the ghost of one, and, tragically, knew it. Her skin had become sallow, and there were deep, hanging folds over her eyes. She had made a graceful, not unsuitable effort to disguise the effect of time; she wore discernible make-up, which she had been careful to blend together, and there was none of the crumby, powdery texture which results on some people when the colours run into the wrinkles. The little hair which showed under a tight-fitting turban was dark, and she was dressed like a bride's mother, with a fur cape over her silk dress, and spikily high heeled shoes. She looked pathetic, an intimation of mortality for that ravishing girl. When she came close to me, I was smothered by a wave of heavy scent.

Mrs Pascoe gushed. She said, 'Oh, Mr Crawford, I'm so sorry, you must forgive me for intruding like this, I know how you must feel—your poor leg, how is it now?—and such a long time that you've been laid up—it must be dreadful for you—'

'Oh, mother,' Jenny murmured.

'Now, Jenny, even if you are cold and unfeeling— naturally I wish to express my sympathy to Mr Crawford, and when he's been so kind to you too.'

Jenny had slumped down on the floor in front of the fire; her chin rested on her knees. Mrs Pascoe burbled on. She admired the view, the furniture, the inscriptions on my plaster cast, and she repeated several times her sympathy for my injuries. It took three quarters of an hour for her to work through her list of appropriate conversation, to which Jenny sulkily listened. I think that the poor woman was made uncomfortable by her unresponsive audience, but she sat on and on. For Jenny's sake I wanted to be kind to her mother. I said at last,

'It is so kind of you to have called. I'm glad to have had the opportunity of meeting you.' But she did not get up. She blushed. As I watched the red stain spread over her neck and forehead, I remembered the delicate colour which came so entrancingly on her daughter's cheeks. But Jenny had developed sophistication before my eyes. I solaced myself with the thought of what lay beneath her clothes.

Mrs Pascoe did not know how to begin. She looked

appealingly at her daughter. 'Jenny—darling—I—'

'Oh, mother,' Jenny said again. It was all she had said since entering the house. She looked at me with a pitying smile. 'My poor mother can't get the words out. But she wants you to know. I'm pregnant.'

I did not know whether the expected reaction was one of congratulation, horror or pity. Did this still count as such a dramatic announcement these days? But one glance at Mrs Pascoe's miserable, embarrassed, disgusted face showed me the answer. I murmured,

'I'm so sorry.'

'Oh, I don't mind,' Jenny said. 'I like babies. It's mamma who is so upset, not me.'

'Well, Jenny, you can hardly expect her—' I said.

I looked at the suffering mother. Suddenly she started speaking, in a gabble of high pitched words.

'I've tried so hard, brought her up so carefully. Oh, Jenny, what did I do wrong? I did everything I could, even your father could never say that I neglected you, so particular we were about your friends and making you come home early in the evening and fetching you from parties, you were such a good little girl always, so pretty and obedient, I don't know why things have changed so much. It was when you started being a student, I knew no good would come of it, you insisted, and Miss Hardy at the High School, she was keen on it. I'm sure you would have done better at a secretarial college, a nice steady job and living at home. It's the boys, that Ian, I always said that we shouldn't let you—but you would move into that house, there wasn't anything I could do, and the professor at the university said they all did it nowa-days—but oh Jenny, Jenny couldn't you at least have been a little careful?' I thought that at least was a fair complaint.

Jenny murmured,

'I didn't do it on purpose.'

'I'm sorry you are so upset,' I said. 'But I'm not quite sure—I mean, is there anything I can do?' As I spoke, I had a sudden idea of what Mrs Pascoe might think I had already done; but no matter what St Paul said that adultery in the heart did to the immortal soul—another of the titbits of education I had derived from the missionary bible—even he did not think that lusting after a woman would make her pregnant.

'Oh, that's just it, Mr Crawford, you must be wondering why we're telling you all this, I'm so ashamed, it's so dreadful to have to admit—but I did not know where else to turn, you have been so kind to Jenny, you have such influence over her. She won't take any notice of anything I say, anything at all. Undutiful, heartless—I'm at my wits' end.'

'Are you trying to persuade Jenny to have an abortion?' I said.

'Oh, no, no, my husband would never—I mean, we don't—no, I never thought she should—well, do that. Not have the baby taken away. Oh dear, it's so dreadful to have to talk about such things, I've always tried so hard not to think about them, I've always said that there are enough beautiful things in the world to rest our thoughts on. One doesn't have to talk about wars and ugliness.'

'My mother is an escapist, Ian says,' Jenny remarked.

'Ian! Don't mention that young man. He's the one, it was him that led you astray in the first place, with his long hair and his messy ways, I knew no good would come of your associating with him.'

'It's Ian's baby, is it?' I asked.

'That doesn't really matter.'

'Oh, Jenny, don't say that, of course it matters, you must think about the future, how are you going to manage all on your own? Oh, I don't know what's to become of us.'

'I must say that I don't see why you are telling me all this, though naturally if I can help in any way ... or perhaps my wife—'

'No, no—it's you, Mr Crawford, Jenny's always talking about you, and you have such knowledge of the world. I used to watch you, such authority you always had. My husband, Jenny's father, that is, he always said that you should be running the country, you always knew where the politicians were going wrong. And Jenny's talked about you such a lot, it's Sylvester this and Sylvester that, I do hope you don't mind her being so cheeky, but I thought you might be able to—I can't do anything with her, and what her father will say ...'

'Haven't you told your father, Jenny?'

'Told her father! Why, she'd be out in the street without a penny to her name if he knew. Oh dear me, that's just the trouble, you see, Mr Pascoe is so strict about these things, he's always brought her up very strictly, I've tried to do that too, though it seems we've failed. Why, he won't even let anyone who's been divorced into the house, stricter than the Royal Enclosure at Ascot, we used to say as a joke. But oh dear me, it's no joke now. He'll never let me see you again, Jenny, not if he finds out.' Mrs Pascoe began, painfully and hideously, to cry. Jenny looked in her mother's bag and found a scented, lace-edged handkerchief, with which she gently mopped her mother's face. Mrs Pascoe snatched it from her, sobbing, and dabbed the tears away herself, wiping delicately under the eyes. She drew some long, shuddering breaths, and with a visible effort, stopped crying, but the tears had destroyed her appearance, her features had in some way dislimned; she looked puffy, cottonwool stuffed, as though, if you poked her cheek, it would retain the finger's impression.

After a long interval, in which I leafed through the *Argus* which lay, much read and re-read, on my table, and in which Jenny gazed serenely out of the window, Mrs Pascoe folded her hands, and spoke in a business like voice.

'I really am sorry, we have wasted such a lot of your time. I don't know what you'll think of us. Look, it's getting dark already, we must have overstayed our welcome. But I should be so glad if I could persuade you to speak to my girl here.'

'Well, yes, anything I can do of course—but what exactly did you want me to say?'

'The silly girl refuses to get married,' Mrs Pascoe said, after forcing herself to the words with a deep breath. But having taken the plunge she found it easier to go on. 'I want her to marry the father, it's

the only thing to do, she wants to keep the baby, but
she says she won't get married, well, you will understand how impossible that is. She's so inexperienced,
she knows nothing of the world, she thinks it's all
free and easy and do-as-you-please, she hasn't any
idea what life is like for an unmarried mother, let
alone for an illegitimate baby—there was a little boy
down the road when you were a child, Jenny, you
wouldn't remember him, little Ned Pearce, it was
so difficult for him, not to mention the family, you
just can't think. If only you'd get married, give the
child a name, give yourself a position in the world,
and your father need never know then either. Oh,
my darling girl, do see reason, do.'

'You want me to persuade Jenny to get married?'

'Yes, she's a good, biddable girl really, she always
has been, always ready to do what she's told, until
now. So I thought that if you spoke to her, since I
don't seem to mean anything to her any more, if
you could use your influence ...' Mrs Pascoe had an
irritatingly plaintive note in her voice, which would
have raised the spirit of opposition in the most bid-
able of children. I said,

'Might it be quite a good idea, Jenny? Would Ian
like it?'

'Ian Macardle!' Mrs Pascoe cried. 'Not him, he
would be worse than no husband. No, it's Toby Norman I want my girl to marry. With the protection
of his name, and his title, nobody could say anything
unkind to her then. Oh Jenny, fancy yourself as a
lady. It would be in all the papers. And you said
that the duke and duchess were so nice to you when

you went there. You'd love it, really. And,' she added, as an afterthought, 'he's such a nice young man. I don't know why you are being so stubborn.'

'But I don't love him, mother.'

'What's that got to do with it—but anyway, you loved him enough to behave like that with him, didn't you? I don't know what's come over you. Mr Crawford, do speak to her.'

'Does Toby want to marry you?' I asked.

'Oh, he'd do it out of kindness. I don't think he wants to marry anybody, but he'd do it for my sake, I should think.'

'There, you see!' said Mrs Pascoe.

'And do you want to marry him?'

'Of course not.' She sounded unexpectedly scornful. 'He's a sweet person, I admire him tremendously, and I'm very fond of him, who wouldn't be?'

'Yes, he's one of the people nobody could possibly dislike.'

'But I don't want to marry somebody young like that. I want to marry—well, I won't say it.'

'Tell us, Jenny, do,' her mother urged. 'It's not that Ian, is it?'

'No, mother, not Ian. I'd like to marry someone like Mr Rochester.' Her voice softened, and she looked soppily out at the sky, leaving me and her mother flabbergasted. We spoke simultaneously.

'Mr Rochester—what do you—?'

'My dear girl, the principal? But you hardly know him, do you?' I said.

'I know him enough. He's so powerful—strong and safe. I feel sort of akin to him.'

'But Jenny—it's not his baby, is it?'

'Does it matter? It could be,' she said. With her mother there, I did not feel that I could ask the vital question, but my experience told me what the answer would be. This was simply a case of hero worship, of the fantasies of an adolescent girl. It seemed to me quite possible that she was not pregnant at all. And yet, this was my Jenny sitting here, the gentle companion of many of my lonely hours, the sweet, pretty, affectionate girl about whom I had myself indulged in many fantasies. This was the young idealist, whose faith and trust in the mission of Toby Norman and Ian Macardle had made me interested in them; how had she changed so much? How, and why? What was there in a man who seemed to me ugly, clumsy, harsh and unfeeling? I thought, it's all in the eye of the beholder. And as I thought, a parallel track in my mind identified the bell which had been ringing; I had been slow to make the connection, considering his surname. I reached out to the pile of Victorian novels by my side. How strange that Jenny should have spoken of her Mr Rochester in that way; how much more truly than I had realised before the parson's daughter had depicted the behaviour of a silly girl. Jane Eyre had felt herself akin to Mr Rochester; she had said, *he took my feelings from my own power and fettered them in his.* It might, but that she was less the mistress of her vocabulary, have been my Jenny speaking.

I said gently, 'But Jenny, have you any reason to think that he feels like that towards you?'

She smiled, and nodded. I felt completely baffled.

This was not something I could cope with, even though Mrs Pascoe sat there looking like a spaniel. I read, but had not the heart to do so aloud, what Jane Eyre had told herself: *It does good to no woman to be flattered by her superior, who cannot possibly intend to marry her. And it is madness in all women to let a secret love kindle within them, which if unreturned and unknown, must devour the life that feeds it* ... But the quotation did not really apply. Rochester was not superior to Jenny. She, with her seraphic innocence was superior to him, by far. What was there in that dark self-seeker to dazzle a girl who knew men like Toby Norman? Had he hypnotised her with his dark eyes? Had his powerful and, I was sure, potentially brutal personality enslaved hers? I felt certain he was not a scrupulous man; if he had been his fictional namesake, he would have had no compunction in taking the woman he professed to love to a bigamous and blasphemous wedding.

No, it was easy to suppose that Lewis Rochester would have felt no qualms at seducing a girl like Jenny. But I found it impossible to imagine that he had ever wanted to. He was not a man to let a momentary inclination jeopardise the ambition of years. He was not the man to have that kind of inclination in the first place. He was, as Thea had overheard his wife say to him, too cold a fish for that.

I wasn't alone in that opinion. I got rid of my Jenny and her mother, and I wasn't going to mention their visit to Thea. It would irritate me to watch her trying to hide her dislike of the girl to avoid up-setting me. But apparently the same subject had been discussed in the senior common room.

CHAPTER SEVEN

It had been a profitable term for Thea, oddly
enough. The members of the university staff who
were not involved in internal politics found themselves with fewer meetings than usual, and sometimes,
when there was a three line whip on a student rally,
nobody would turn up to be taught. In her tiny
office in the corner of the trefoil tower which housed
arts subjects, Thea was less disturbed than in her
previous terms at Buriton. She had started almost
idly to do some preliminary work on an article due
the next year, meaning not to waste the spare half-
hours, and almost without noticing it she found that
her pile of index cards was growing, and the scheme
for a book was forming in her mind. She hadn't
meant to get tied up with any major work at the
moment. She had always thought that she could
only write when uninterrupted weeks were promised.
But by the middle of term it was clear that the article
was more like a chapter, and the scheme for the next
dozen was clear in her head.

Thea was lucky that her department's secretary was
able to run it. Mrs Tobias was an experienced woman

who recognised the throes of scholastic creation when she saw them, and had the tact not to replace volumes of journals on the shelves or to rearrange the papers piled on Thea's desk. But Thea did not really admit to herself what she was doing until she happened to hear Mrs Tobias on the telephone one day telling a caller that the professor could not speak, she was working on her book. It was ironic that in her academic position she felt that it was guilty self-indulgence to be working at research rather than administration or teaching. Mrs Tobias at least had preserved the old fashioned idea of universities as centres of research. She looked almost disapproving of the waste of time when Thea said she was going across for coffee.

The senior common room was crowded. In the students' union a mass meeting to plan action in detail was going on. Hubert Dale claimed that many students were attending the meeting to protest against the campaign. He was sure that the majority of the young people in Buriton wanted nothing more than to be left alone to get on with their work. Alfred O'Connor was not so sure.

'They mean it this time,' he insisted. 'It's all being master minded by Macardle from his cell.' Very few of the members of the staff were able to feel as detached as Thea. The students' activities affected their working lives and futures. 'Well, he's only on remand, technically innocent. He gets visited. And of course he gets special treatment. You can imagine what an outcry there would be from the do-gooders if a student was treated like a criminal.'

'He hasn't been found guilty,' a young man said.

'Those who insist on legal rights being upheld are not at fault,' Professor Prothero called. 'Do-gooder is not a term of abuse.'

'Nor is it other than proper for people in our position to be sympathetic to the young,' an elderly woman remarked, with a reproving glare at Professor O'Connor.

'Ask the principal!' the same young man said loudly, and subsided giggling amongst his friends. It must have been difficult for men of the old school like Alfred O'Connor to regard these young people as colleagues. With their beards and denims and general air of being there to smash idols, Thea thought, they would be as alien to him as the most left wing students.

'Do you know what that was about?' Thea asked Hubert Dale. He glanced at her above his coffee cup with one eyebrow raised, and Thea remembered that he had been an inspired gossip in the old days. He had ears, Sylvester said, like a field of corn.

'You haven't heard about little Jenny Pascoe?' he asked.

'Heard what?'

'Well, of course my dear, she's the most attractive creature on the campus—present company excepted. A man's girl all through,' Hubert said, giving his high pitched titter. Thea thought that the enclosed academic community in which Hubert lived had done him no good. She used to like him better.

'Sylvester's devoted to her,' she said drily.

'And not the only one, it seems. Have you heard

she's pregnant? Mary Dobson, she's in her college you know, had a visit from her mother. And you'll never guess who—'

'One of those two boys, presumably,' Thea said.

'One would have thought so. But she claims—' He bent his head and whispered the principal's name. Thea was relieved, because she had been fearing that the girl had named Sylvester, unreasonable though it would have been to do so; and her reaction to the other suggestion was equally incredulous. She laughed, and said, 'How ridiculous. Poor girl. I thought she was behaving oddly when I last saw her.'

'Why do you say it's ridiculous?' Hubert looked disappointed.

'Well—you don't believe it, do you? A silly girl who has had her head turned by being given a lift in someone's car. It's all in her mind. The girl's a hysteric.'

'You think so? I suppose you may be right.'

'Oh, yes, I've come across it before. They convince themselves of the truth of their own fantasies. It doesn't always go so far, but it's not unusual. When I was a kid myself I had a pash on the music master. I used to have long imaginary conversations with him. It became embarrassing when we met because I tended to forget that I didn't really know him at all well. I'd take a bet that's what's wrong with Jenny Pascoe. She may not even be pregnant.'

'You may well be right, Thea,' Hubert said. 'Certainly I'd have thought that he was too cold a fish for such rashness. He's always seemed to me the sort of man who doesn't really know that anyone else exists.'

'What about his wife?'

'Joyce? Ah well. You know about her.'

'I've met her a couple of times, and thought she was a very live wire. It was hard to see how those two would ever have got together in the first place, I'll say that much.'

'She's attractive, isn't she? That's what our Jenny's papa thinks too, at least according to Jenny. She told Mary Dobson that Joyce Rochester and Desmond Pascoe are just waiting for the right moment. She said that Lewis knows all about it, and Mrs Pascoe too.'

'So what are they waiting for? After all, divorce by consent—'

'Dearest Thea, what an innocent academic you are. I'm glad you've never had to investigate how one gets rid of a spouse! You have to live apart for two years to divorce by consent, to prove that the marriage has broken down for good; the word the lawyers use is irretrievably. Otherwise you have to prove that it's broken down because of adultery or cruelty, or something equally messy and scandalous. Well, none of that would do an ambitious head of university any good, would it—certainly not as long as he lives in the same place that knows all about his moral shortcomings. And the same applies with knobs on to a pillar of the Methodist community like Pascoe— local preacher, councillor, all that. He couldn't do it and stay where he was. It would probably even affect his business. Take Freeman's Common for instance; the council wouldn't admit to anything but business considerations, and proper planning for the area and so on, but they're only human—too damned human, some of them. Though by the way, did you hear that Rochester wants to withdraw the university tender, and use the registry site instead?'

'Hubert, it can't be true.' Thea sipped her coffee, and pushed the half full cup away; it was bitter and cold. 'Nowadays nobody thinks twice about divorce. I should think half the people I know have been married more than once. Universities are full of professors who have left wives and kids behind in the suburbs and gone off with a pretty student.'

'You're thinking in terms of London, my dear. We're old fashioned in the provinces. And even universities—they want to choose pretty carefully when they are appointing people to run them. It's just one of those things, it's the way the world is. I'm all in favour of it, actually. I'm becoming very moral in my old age.' Hubert's face was both prim and smug, the mask of the conformist. It was hard to remember him as the witty undergraduate who had exchanged jokes with Sylvester beside the Cherwell.

'But Hubert, what's the point of people sticking together if they don't want to? Without small children, there's no virtue in it.'

'You can't have your cake and eat it. But Rochester can leave Joyce for a couple of years if he moves away. If the Northern University took him, he could arrive there as a grass widower. After all, she's got her career in Buriton.'

'And the Pascoes?'

'Well, I don't know. Perhaps after the Freeman's Common question has been decided— Look, Thea, here's the great man himself. He doesn't often come in here these days.'

Rochester queued behind a couple of young women at the counter for his cup of coffee. He was wearing his gown, and under its black folds his shoulders jutted wide and square. He carried himself like a guardsman.

'Was he in the army?' Thea asked Hubert.

'Yes, but we don't talk about it—he wasn't commissioned. It's regarded as tactless to mention his past around here.'

'Really? I thought he was a barrister or something.'

'Unsuccessfully. No briefs. I'm told he attributes it to his lack of connections. If he'd been sent to school over here, instead of in the States—he's Canadian originally. That's why their boy is away at school, sent off with his teddy at the age of seven, so that he'll know the right people.'

'Hubert, you sound awfully uncharitable.'

Hubert Dale laughed a little self consciously. 'I'm sorry for the wretched kid. Anne and I decided to keep ours at home, you know, and I'm sure they benefit more from their family environment—but of course we have four. It's different for Clovis.' Thea had not taken Hubert Dale's remarks personally. Like many of the people she and Sylvester had known since their principles had been abstract, Hubert felt the need to justify the actions which circumstances forced upon him. She did not feel like hearing again the list of the benefits of state education and day schools.

Rochester looked around the room, and moved over to the table where the younger members of the sociology department were lounging. He spoke in

134

a low voice to them, and in a moment the three young people went out of the room. Rochester stood looking around; it was a long room in the university staff club, furnished with battered modern elegance and adorned by good lithographs. It was open to more members than those who were on the teaching staff of the university but at this time in the morning there were no outsiders present, and Rochester rapped his signet ring against the glass of the low table. Slowly conversations ceased and everyone looked at him.

'Ladies and gentlemen,' he said, 'forgive me for interrupting you. It seems a good moment—I think we're all discreet here.' He smiled at the professor of sociology, Prothero, and it became clear why he had found an errand for the younger sociologists, who were well known to be more on the side of the students than the staff. 'I think our young friends are working up to renewed action,' he went on. 'We've had quite a lull, but Macardle's case is to be heard on Monday. I thought I'd just remind you, and suggest that it might be an idea to take any personal files home. You'll know what I mean.'

Alfred O'Connor stood up, small and almost absurd beside the principal, but with the dignity of outrage. 'Are you implying that the students of this university are planning what they call a sit-in?'

'I draw my deductions, as you can,' Rochester said. He sat down and started to fill his pipe with meticulous attention.

'And you intend to allow this? You won't do any-thing about it?'

'What would you suggest?'

'There are laws in this country, I believe.'

'There is no law which prevents a student from entering a building in his own university.'

'And their friends? You must know that they have been inciting students to come from all over the country.'

'It's a thorny point, legally,' Rochester said. He spoke quietly, but everyone was listening. 'The students of Buriton aren't trespassers in their own campus. If they invite their friends presumably they aren't trespassers either. In any case, it's not a criminal offence. I don't think the police would be willing to intervene, until there's a breach of the peace threatened. And if we leave them alone there won't be.'

Thea went across to her room in the arts tower. As she walked past the students' union she could hear the sounds of voices and cheering, muffled through the ventilation grilles. There were very few students on the campus, though two boys were standing with a sheaf of leaflets near the entrance, presumably to direct latecomers to the mass meeting. The manager of the university bookshop was supervising his assistant in screwing the shutters over the windows. He said, laughing, 'Early closing today,' as Thea went past. Mrs Tobias was working her way through a pile of the usual administrative queries and requests. Thea paused on the way through her room, and said, 'I'm going early today. Would you like to go off too?'

'Thank you, but I'll just finish this. I'll lock up

after you. Nobody else has come in today and there hasn't been a sign of the tutorial class. I don't know what this place is coming to.'

Thea packed the notes for her book into her brief-case. Not much point in locking the filing drawers. Two keys would open every cabinet in the building. She went out to her car with a load of books and map rolls, and went back for her case and card index box. She looked around the little room; an olive green carpet, wall to wall because she was a professor; grey metal desk and orange chromium and canvas chair; nothing, she thought, that she gave a damn for. 'They are welcome to the lot,' she muttered.

People were beginning to filter out from their meeting into the chilly sunshine. The groups of students fell silent as Thea approached, and when she had passed they started giggling, and muttering together. She felt quite gay at the thought of leaving for the duration, as it were. She would set up her desk in the so far unused upstairs drawing-room of the little house; she knew exactly what the next two chapters should say and would enjoy setting it on paper.

An enormous, shabby and rusty estate car was parked beside hers in the car park. The mini would almost have fitted into its back, which was in fact occupied by two vociferous golden retrievers, bashing themselves against the wire grid which prevented them from jumping forward. At Thea's approach they launched themselves noisily at the windows.

'They only want to be friendly.' The driver got out and apologised to Thea for her animals' aggression.

She was a tall woman who had once been beautiful, battered now like her motor car, but undaunted. Thea smiled and shook her head, and put her packages in the back of the mini. 'I'll just back a bit so that you can—oh, there he is at last. Toby, darling, you've been ages!' Toby Norman was coming towards them, his head haloed by the sun. The likeness was clear between his mother and himself. He came up to her and put his arm round her shoulder, and said,

'Sorry, ma. It went on a bit. Did you meet Professor Crawford? This is my mother.'

'I'm taking this silly boy home,' the duchess explained. 'Enough is enough, we thought.'

'How will they manage without him?' Thea said, smiling. Indeed, it was hard to envisage a Buriton demo without him leading it. Were there eager revolutionaries ready to step into the gap left by Toby and by Ian Macardle?

'They're getting on all right,' he said shortly. 'Too well by half, in fact. Shut up, dogs.'

'You—er, don't want to take part in whatever they're planning?'

'I think Toby's had enough,' his mother said. 'We didn't mind when it was a matter of principle, we couldn't have stopped him then anyway. That did no harm. But criminal offences are another matter. All that Toby's friends are fussing about now is the due processes of the law being used against a student.'

'That's the trouble,' he explained, a frown on his once smooth brow. 'After all, we were fighting to end the privileges that students had, because there were so few of us and so many of the rest who didn't have our advantages. Well, you know what it was about, when we started. At the beginning of term, you know. I still believe in it. But they don't seem to listen so much now that Ian's not there. All they want is to get him out of prison and stop the trial going on, they want him to have the very privileges that we said we shouldn't have if the others didn't. I mean, they wouldn't let out anyone else without trying them, would they?'

'Toby's got to come back and give evidence next week,' his mother said. 'But I think a couple of days away will do him good.'

'But did Ian set fire to the registry?' Thea said. 'I thought you all said he didn't.'

'I don't know,' he said roughly. His face looked like paper which has been thrown away and smoothed out again, no longer the mask of a young god, but a worried, not very clever young man who had lost his faith. 'I didn't see anything, I was in the Black Maria with Jenny and the others. Anyone could have got in round the back and fixed it up. You can get phosphorus in any lab if you want.'

'Phosphorus?'

'Well, it's easier to get than explosives, isn't it? You'd need more than a match.'

'Dearest boy, what should Professor Crawford and I know about methods of arson? What indeed, do you?'

Toby looked as nearly sulky as he could. 'Any schoolboy could tell you. It's the only self igniting thing I can think of, anyway. And Peter Petrov said that the fuzz had been nosing round the labs asking questions.'

'Does Ian know anything about chemistry?' Thea asked. 'I thought he was reading law.'

'We all do A levels in something.' He brushed the passenger seat of the estate car free of cellophane sweet wrappings and folded himself on to it.

'He does sulk, you know,' the duchess said to Thea. 'But it doesn't last. He's a sweet natured boy, too much so really. Some of his friends, some of the young people he has brought down to stay—we haven't known what to do with them. But he means so well. He's always been such a kind child. He was the head of his gang, you can imagine, no matter where he was, but he never bullied them, never threw his weight around. Aren't children a worry?' She sat in the car, and started the engine. At the noise, the dogs instantly lay down and were quiet. 'Anyway, it's a mercy that Toby wasn't with his friends on the obstruction charge. He's longing to go to the States, and you know what the Yanks are like about visas for people with criminal records.'

'Are you longing to go to America, Toby?' Thea asked, surprised. He looked embarrassed, and his mother explained.

'It's a peace centre. Something to do with Gandhi, and Luther King—I can't follow it all myself, but Toby's been promised a place. A conviction would have been the end.'

'I suppose so.'

'You must come to Norman yourself. My husband's family has always been closely associated with the

140

university here. Dear kind Lewis Rochester! And my husband was the chancellor until last year. We'll look forward to it.' She smiled brilliantly, as if for a camera; and the big car shot away, scattering gravel behind it.

CHAPTER EIGHT

I'd been irritated, earlier in the year, by Bernard Trent urging me to take an interest in local events, but I suppose if once, then always a political animal. Or did I want to please Jenny? She had suggested that I should write about Buriton too. That was the only time she mentioned Rochester to me, just after she had met him properly for the first time as a student in his university, rather than as the child of a friend. He had even asked her about me, having she said, picked her up in his car as she was leaving our house. She did not have much to tell him at the time. Her initial kindness was almost impersonal, and I wasn't, I later realised, so much a person as an object of charity. It was painful to know that in retrospect.

She had told him that she did not know whether I was much changed, never having watched me on television, and he had been surprised, and said, perhaps for repetition, that I had an acute political mind, honed to its sharpness by an interest in all minor details of human behaviour. Jenny repeated this titbit, at a time when I was blind to all humans except myself, as she might have given me a bunch of grapes. It was a precursor to what she thought her own brilliant solution to my problem, and she was pleased with herself for having the idea of turning my mind to such small scale politics as were available. To her, of course, Buriton was the whole world. I did not tell her that what Lewis Rochester wanted was for me to concentrate on him.

I could not take an interest in anybody then, least of all the administrator of a small university. But as the time went by accidie receded. Buriton and its personalities were no more attractive, but when had I ever been fond of my subjects? After all, does a surgeon love the cringing flesh?

But curiosity returned before judgment. When Thea arrived home early on the day that the students' occupation of the university's buildings began, I was seething at the first rejection my writing had had since I was nineteen; not a printed slip, naturally, and it came in the form of suggestions for a few amendments. But Bernard Trent did not want the article I had written. It was, of all things, too right wing. I didn't display enough sympathy, he complained, to the students; he spread the best butter thick, and praised the analysis of events, saying that political events were like iron filings to Sylvester Crawford's magnet. If I could just change the emphasis of the opinion paragraph, and say a little less about the adolescent petulance of their demands, then he would be delighted to print it, with the prominence my name deserved.

I showed the letter to Thea. 'Damn it all,' I said,

'you can respect a demonstrator whose target is an oppressor on a national scale. But look how their horizons have dwindled here. They don't ask anything for people who need something any more. And Bernard says I'm fascist to deride them. I think you are wasting your time on that lot.'

'Not today. They are battening down for a siege up the hill. Not that I mind, I've plenty of work to get on with. I suppose it's good healthy fun and an education for life and all that.'

'Their lives won't consist of demos once they've got a living to earn,' I growled.

'You never know. After all, Sylvester, we were marching from Aldermaston quite a long time after coming from Oxford.'

'That wasn't the same thing.'

'It was a demo, really, just by another name. And you know, I agree with what Bernard implies in that letter. It's a poor look out if they aren't radical and full of protest when they are young; if the students like the system now they'll be rabid authoritarians by the time they are middle aged. Couldn't you just tone it down a bit? Leave out the bit about the long term interests of scholarship and acceptance of intellectual disciplines.'

'I'm damned if I will. This whole business stinks, Thea, take it from me. There's something in it for someone.'

'What on earth do you mean?' Thea was preoccupied. She was unpacking her briefcase, reading the papers she took out of it and putting them in separate piles. She had not mentioned that she was writing a book, but obviously there wasn't much point in trying to discuss anything less than forty centuries old with her at the moment, and I was not, in fact, anxious to stumble into words with my nebulous feeling that all was not as it seemed in Buriton, and that what I had heard the students saying recently did not ring true. It seemed to me as though the instigators of the activity were urging it on for its own sake. We had not heard much since the beginning of term about the original demand that higher education should be free for all, and I could not believe that any student really supposed that Ian Macardle, having been charged, would be released without a trial. They were using his arrest as a peg to hang a demonstration on, and I could not think why. There might be money in it for Desmond Pascoe, perhaps, but that was just lucky for him. Certainly every day that the students continued disrupting the little town, the less likely its representatives were to be eager for the university's expansion. And, by this time, the end of March, disruption there certainly was.

As the *Guardian* said, giving Buriton the honour of a leading article in early March, student militancy tends to reach a climax during the early months of the year. It meant, let it ride and by next term all will be forgotten. A portentous academic whose Radio 3 broadcast was reprinted in the *Listener* chided the administration of Buriton for not having been sufficiently adaptable and conciliatory; he was a sociologist from East Anglia. But the *Daily Telegraph* congratulated Lewis Rochester on taking a stand which it described as long overdue in the annals of the British student movement.

Bernard Trent published an article under his own name in the *Argus*, instead of mine, and discussed the wider issues of youthful revolt and the restructuring of society in the context.

If the supply of newspapers and other essentials reached the embattled students no doubt they were gratified to be paid so much attention.

The siege began the afternoon of the day that Thea and those of her colleagues who had been equally prudent brought essential and private papers home. The four tower blocks on the campus were occupied by forces of Buriton students. That was the Friday, and they were joined over the weekend by bus loads from other universities. The coaches parked in our road and I watched the reinforcements marching with sleeping bags instead of rifles on their shoulders up the hill. The uniformed porters of the university were standing beside the campus gates, but made no attempt to repel raiders. They would, in fact, have had no legal right to do so, for each group was met and formally invited in by one of the Buriton leaders. All went peacefully; that is to say, without aggression, but with a certain amount of good natured noise. At this time the whole thing was a lark on a giant scale.

Tim Gifford came in on the Saturday, and seemed amused by what he saw from the window. After all, as he said, he was of the generation which knocked off bobbies' helmets on Boat Race night. He told me that the free side show was good for me and that I was getting on splendidly. Indeed, in another few days

I might start walking gently about the house. The physiotherapist would come on Monday and make sure that I hadn't lost the use of my good leg and teach me to use crutches. I was distressed to find that the prospect of long awaited release from immobility filled me with more apprehension than pleasure.

I wondered whether any of the visiting students would try to camp out on the common, but they kept well within their legal rights, and did nothing that was not permitted. They did not even pause on the pavements, and I noticed that whenever a group of them stopped in the street to talk one of their marshals came to shepherd them on. They were entitled, like anyone else, to use the public highway for passing along, and so they did, up and down to the shops with arms full of tinned baked beans or cylinders of bottled gas.

They spent the weekend settling in. It was usually a quiet time anyway, except in the library and the laboratories, and those two buildings were left to the troglodytes who wanted to work, so that there was no actual disruption of teaching for those two days. But the congregation of young people with a cause was disturbing by its very existence, and though I could not see the tower blocks from my window, I was told that all their windows, visible from a lot of the rest of the town, and from out to sea, were plastered with notices and slogans. Every can of spray paint in the town had been sold.

The slogans were elementary and offensive, and the demands of the demonstrators, presented in due form to the principal, were simple. They wanted

147

higher grants and an egalitarian society, and the heat taken off Ian Macardle.

At first it seemed as undirected a show of strength as any I'd seen; the heat could hardly be taken off Macardle, or the prosecution case dropped, by the university authorities against whom the action was being taken.

After three nights, the signs of over occupation were disagreeably in evidence. Litter fluttered from the upper windows of the towers, coming to rest in the trees of the arboretum which surrounded them. A copper beech tree, nearly in leaf, was whitened as though by blossom with discarded tissues. It was only too easy to imagine the squalor of the rooms inside.

On the Monday things were still friendly and almost jaunty. The students went out for walks, and some, carrying rolls of towel, to swim. The principal drove up, and parleyed; and drove away.

The next day his statement was published in the national papers, that he was making no offers or promises. One of the daily papers had received a communiqué from the occupying power, to the effect that the students would indefinitely squat in the university premises. Nothing was said as to what they would do after and if Macardle was convicted: were they going to sleep on office floors for ever?

Rochester's answer was on the radio and television news the same afternoon. The students could stay as long as they felt like it. All members of the staff had already removed what they needed. Any further inconvenience, he said, would cause later generations of students to suffer more than anyone else. The staff were going to have a break with pay, and the principal expected that more original work would be published by the teaching staff of Buriton than for years before. If they couldn't teach they could do research, and fulfil the prime function of a community of scholars, who needed only pencil and paper, he said. The tower blocks were an extra they could manage without.

The dampening effect of this statement was well judged, though as Thea said, it was not true. She met her colleagues when she went shopping in the town, sitting disconsolately in cafes, or wandering aimlessly along the streets. There were many who had taken no notice of Rochester's warning to remove their valuables, and more who had never got the message. However, most of them agreed that it had been a good move, in diplomatic terms. It would not be nearly such fun for the students to occupy the university, if nobody minded.

They had started picketing the site, though to their own detriment. Heating oil and food supplies were turned away at the gates, none of the drivers delivering them caring in the least if he could not do so. It was all quite without acrimony. They kept the dust carts out, also, and Thea said that at the top of the hill the smell of decaying refuse was beginning to be noticeable.

I could imagine the scene inside. It wouldn't be much different from others I had reported on in the past. Some of the students would display the nesting instinct even in these circumstances, turning an office into a home from home, folding up blankets in the morning and cleaning their teeth at night. But most of them would throw themselves with glee into dis-organisation, welcoming a chance to camp in corri-dors, cook in classrooms, piss out of the window and celebrate anarchy. How times had changed.

In the days when the young still worked for global ideals I marched with the nuclear disarmers from Aldermaston to Trafalgar Square. I'd been sent as a reporter, but I supported the campaign's aims, and many of my friends were there. We were of the genera-tion which had still done compulsory national service and many of us had experience of living rough. It was at a time before the roads of the world were dotted with the young carrying their sleeping equip-ment tortoise-like on their backs. A few of us had khaki sleeping bags, but the equipment most people had for the night was a hairy grey blanket and a pillow case to stuff their clothes in. We slept in orderly rows on the board floors of school or village halls, and cooked up for supper with an army-taught economy of labour.

I suddenly wondered, looking back at those days of enthusiasm, whether the feeling of them came so clearly into my mind because I was now ex-periencing a particular rage which had not overcome me since then. That April in Berkshire I thought I had an observer's detachment—until, as we would put it now, I lost my cool. Today in Buriton, below my surface amusement, overcoming my lethargy and surging up from my deepest self was a bubble of fury at the awareness of cynicism manipulating ideals. I hadn't realised that I cared, let alone how much. With the anger came an impersonal satisfaction. My friends would be pleased, I thought, to know that I was back in life.

Marching with us that year, to protest against nuclear weapons, was our friend Stefan Czernin. He is the manager of one of the national charitable foundations now. He had left all his family behind and we have learnt that they are thriving; but we didn't know it then. He might, so far as he knew at the time, have committed them all to suffering when he escaped across a frozen minefield. But he hoped that their lives were going on in the terror that had become normality for his parents and that his sisters were too young to mind.

The night's stop was in a suburban primary school. We staked out our corners under a collage of Easter chickens and went along to the pub. We were odd-men-out in the lounge bar, naturally, bearing with us the aura of protest and rocking the boat and un-thinkable wars. Thea was not with us. She had just recovered from her second miscarriage and was to join the rally at Trafalgar Square. But my posterity was much in my thoughts.

Stefan and I, and two or three other marchers, withdrew to a corner with our half pints, feeling grubby and unwelcome. The bar was full of glossy youngish men in blazers and silk cravats, who were discussing the march. They thought it a damned cheek for us to invade their village. One of the phrases they bandied about was 'Bloody conshies', a slang term out of date even then, which meant pacifists who had conscientious objections to military service. I had been, as it happened in Palestine with the

Gunners, and Roy James who was with us, had served in Korea.

'Want to hand us all over to the commies,' one of the men said. He thrust his sweating pink face towards Stefan who was sitting the nearest to him. 'No better than commies yourselves. If you like it so much why don't you go back there? Go behind the iron curtain?' Stefan stared at him without answering, his pale eyes like marbles. The man gulped down the rest of his whisky and bawled an order for more. His friends were watching him with the anxiety of Englishmen who fear that somebody is going to make a scene. A slightly older man said nervously,

'Come on, John, old chap. Betty will be waiting.'

'I can't understand you people,' the man called John said. I stood up, disliking the alcoholic breath that gusted downwards into my face. 'The best weapon our country has ever had and you want us to give it away. I don't know.'

'After all,' Roy James said mildly, 'we can't use it.'

'Why not? Why the hell not? We bloody well can. We bloody well will, if I know anything about it. I'm a reserve pilot, a pilot in the Air Force. We'll use it if I get my finger near the button. Better be dead than red, that's what I say, better dead than red.'

I was more sensitive than Stefan, who did not instantly envisage his own family dead instead of red. I realised that almost at once. But a gust of anger clenched my muscles before reason loosed them and, as I had never believed was possible, almost without intending it, I had bashed my fist into the other man's chin. The brawl went no further, for the resident's friends and mine hustled their champions away. But I could, briefly, have killed a man.

I think it was the last time I have felt such a spasm of hatred, but perhaps it was just as well for me as a journalist to know what it was. I was ashamed now of even feeling the ghost of that passion. But when I watched the Buriton students, I despised them in a way, for the calculation of their anger.

Student sit-ins were almost part of the great tradition of British education, but this seemed to be the first time that nobody had admitted to caring. It must have been very disconcerting for the ring leaders. To camp uncomfortably in the towers of Buriton, without pleas and blandishments to come out, or to state terms, or even to parley, seemed a little farcical. By the middle of the week, some of the faint hearted could be seen slinking away from the campus, trying to look casual. Even Professor Prothero, by some wile of the principal, had been muzzled. Rochester telephoned or called on his professors and asked them to spread the word to their junior staff, that everything was going according to his plan and nobody was to worry. He did stress to a carefully chosen reporter that the university would stand firm next term also. Only those whose examination papers were up to standard would receive degrees. No allowances would be made for missed work or destroyed notes. Exams were by then only two months away.

One adapts very quickly to new ways of living. After three or four days it seemed natural and invariable to have the campus under occupation. Thea went upstairs to work as automatically as if she had not been going to her office for years.

The news media, too, were becoming bored, and both the massive camera trailers and the squads of men with apparatus had gone to more exciting targets by the middle of the week. Only the local papers sent their regular news hounds. I knew one of them, Dick Harker, who left Fleet Street when his paper folded and discovered happiness in the provinces. He used to be a thin, wrinkled pippin of a man, wracked by stomach ache. After five years on the *Buriton Packet*, he stood upright and had got fat. Dick had tried to interview me when I first came, and I'd sent him off angrily. Now I was pleased to see him, and beckoned him in.

'How's the progress report?' I asked.

'What, up the hill? I dunno—much the same probably. They aren't doing any harm, so there's not much for me to write about. As you know, Sylvester.'

'So what are you doing?'

'It's the town council's meeting tonight. I'm just getting a reminder of Freeman's Common—soon to be Wage Slave's Paradise. You wait till you see the area of soft-selling floor space Desmond Pascoe is going to cram into that acre.'

'You're so sure that the students' behaviour has finished the university's hopes?'

'Didn't you know? The university has withdrawn its tender. It's all just a formality now. The old ducks will quack on about being a partner with commerce in a great enterprise—the town isn't selling, just letting the developer use the ground, for some nugatory sum. But of course, that's all talk.'

'I suppose the university wanted to avoid the humiliation of being turned down,' I said. 'They would have been, don't you think? The student disorders couldn't have worked out better from Pascoe's point of view.'

'Yeah—some of us wondered if he'd fixed it, as a matter of fact. His daughter's involved, after all. But no, the university has put in an application for permission to build on the site of the old house. They made damn sure it couldn't be repaired by bulldozing the ruins saying they weren't safe, so now there's nothing to say no. They'd been refused permission to demolish in the past.'

'So it's all turning out very neatly.'

'Yeah. And Buriton loses one of the only open spaces left. But I guess it's all according to plan. The only question is—whose?'

I wondered too who was driving; I could almost hear the wheels go round. And though I was practised at understanding myself, I was uncharacteristically having trouble in deciding whether hatred for people who set up as chauffeurs of human affairs outweighed my apathy about their destination.

I'd changed: recently, in returning to life, and over the last years in my attitude to it. My articles written even five years before showed a committed, if critical interest in the human machinery. Then I accepted the need for its existence. But long illness had engendered, or perhaps exposed, a distrust of the pollution of worldliness. No one, I thought, should manipulate another.

Men like Lewis Rochester used that word with pride.

He dropped in one Sunday with his wife and son. They had been walking up from the university church and met Thea and Clovis in the street. My family had been kite flying. Edward Rochester and Clovis stared at each other like hostile dogs. But their instant suspicion annoyed their mothers who sent them out at once with a football. They slouched along to the common, hands in pockets, walking well apart.

'Aren't little boys funny!' Joyce Rochester said with a light laugh. She was as small and thin as Thea, but with reddened hair short and waved around her head, and a dress and coat of extremely conventional smartness, looked a very different sort of person. She was skilful with her cosmetics, but they showed. Thea wears layers of unguents too, but you wouldn't know it. I felt violently uninterested in Mrs Rochester, and had to remind myself that minor characters in my life were not so in their own.

Lewis Rochester propped his bottom on the windowsill. The sun was on his back, and his shadow fell across my lap.

Joyce and Thea confronted each other warily, hackles raised like their sons'. They had both learnt the small talk of civilisation and like my sister who could talk washing machines to any army wife, they knew how to make the right noises. But one might have expected them to get on; they had a lot in common, that pair of high powered women.

'I've seen you on television and admired you so much,' Mrs Rochester said to me. 'What a pity you—

are you planning to go back to it?'

'Yes,' I said. Thea looked at me in surprise, and then smiled with a brief, intimate brilliance.

'He can do a piece on you, Principal,' she said gaily. Rochester smiled, and started to light his pipe. The match flame was reflected in his dark eyes, his teeth were strong and white, and I thought, *'All the better to eat you with, my dear.'* He'd be the wolf, in an encounter between us.

'Mr Crawford has bigger fish to fry,' Joyce Rochester said. Her glance slid coldly over her husband. Yet one could see why she must once have loved him. Thea clearly found him attractive, perhaps for the very qualities I disliked in him, the powerful, self confident force of the man. 'You know,' Joyce said, 'I knew the people who used to live here. They had the prettiest drawing-room in Buriton—the big room upstairs.'

'Would you like to see it?' Thea asked. The two women went upstairs together. Rochester looked out of the window.

'There's old Pascoe,' he said. 'Measuring up.'

'I don't know him.'

'Over there, in chapel clothes. He'll have been preaching. Interesting fellow. Self made, but none the worse for that. He has a social worker's instinct.'

'I thought he was a developer.'

'Oh, professionally. And he does well out of it, no doubt of that. But he's very public spirited, within the limits of Buriton. We're alike in a way, Pascoe and I. We're both manipulators.'

'You're proud of that?'

'It's only a word. Though it's what all social workers do—they persuade people to do what would be best for them as though they had decided to themselves. Manipulating individuals for their own good. I'm working for groups of individuals for the greater good, in my trade. It is a difference of degree.'

'That's how you see the job of running a university, is it?' I asked.

'That—or any other institution, if one wants to leave a mark on it. After all, it's simply a matter of one person seeing further than the rest. It's what I'm paid to do.'

'You need to know what the others want.'

'Well, for heaven's sake, you've seen enough of that. Every politician, or doctor, even every parish councillor reckons to know what other people want, or need, better than they do themselves. To deny that is as hypocritical as despising personal ambition. How would we ever get a prime minister without it? I don't like false modesty. I'm an élitist.'

Clovis and Edward had joined a group of boys who were trying to make a go-cart work. Edward was a weedy child, and stood back while Clovis wielded a screwdriver. 'Are you educating your son to lead?' I asked.

'He's down for Eton, if that's what you mean. I hope he'll build on that foundation.'

'Did you have that sort of education?'

'Alas, no. My father was an English business man running the Canadian branch of his firm. I was sent to a Jesuit school where I got a good classical education but none of the right contacts.'

'I didn't realise you were a Catholic.'

'I'm not,' he said. 'It was just the best school in the place.'

Joyce Rochester and Thea came downstairs chatting amiably, but I could see that Thea was as pleased as I, when the Rochesters drained their glasses of sherry and left. Thea laughed when they had gone.

'You'll never guess what her factory is going in for now,' she said. She started clearing the table, and handed me the oil and vinegar, and egg yolks in a copper bowl. I started mixing mayonnaise. 'She's going to make plastic garden ornaments.'

'Gnomes?' I asked.

'No, granite crosses! You know, like this.' She showed me some photographs in one of her books, round-faced Maltese crosses roughly engraved on stone pillars. Apparently these relics of the distant past were scattered around Cornwall. 'She's taken a mould and they'll be expensive extras for high class gardens. Isn't it marvellous?' This tit-bit had put Thea into a very good temper and she whistled as she cut up tomatoes.

'Which ones are the Jesuits, Thea?' I said. 'Are they the ones that say the end justifies the means? Or is that a different lot?'

Thea, who never read fiction, had hoards of unrelated factual information in her head.

'Those are the ones,' she said. 'St Thomas Aquinas. Why?'

'I just wondered.'

'We used to have debates about it at school. I always spoke against it, and lost every time. Can you tap on the window for Clovis? If the mayonnaise is ready we could have lunch.' I beckoned our son and watched his sensible, un-introspective mother with affection. She didn't worry about the ends and her means were honest. I hoped all universities were full of people like her.

CHAPTER NINE

Thea was always amused by the self-importance of the law. In magistrates' courts its dignity, she thought, was minimal: smallish rooms, always too hot or too cold, furnished with uncomfortable and badly made furniture, either light or dark stained oak; three justices of the peace of a lack of distinction that was incongruous below the coat of arms. But she liked to think that she was becoming less intellectually arrogant as she grew older. It was, no doubt, a good theory that an average citizen should be able to impress generally accepted standards and theories upon the law. Its professionals perhaps lived in too rarefied an atmosphere to dispense understanding as well as justice.

In Buriton's crown court in this last week of March, a high court judge was sitting, Sir John Withycombe, formerly a rebel barrister of some renown, who spent a lucrative career battering against the barriers of illiberal convention. He first became famous outside the Inns of Court by defending the translation of a classical gem of explicit lust. Thea had met him when he was doing his best to prevent the deportation of one of her African students who faced certain torture and death in his own country. He had taken a great fancy to Thea and they used to meet very decorously for lunch in a famous fish restaurant. He had talked for a long time about the living death it would be on the bench, and how he would never consent to the muzzle that such a position would put on him. He used to play with the idea of leaving the Bar for academic life, or to direct a charitable foundation. In the end, he told his friends, his children had persuaded him to accept with gratitude the moment he was offered the step up, and he turned out to enjoy his new job, working on prejudice from within, as he liked to think, by imposing minimum sentences for such crimes as using soft drugs, and punishing offences against the person with far more severity than those against property. He admitted himself that his experience and character had not made him very well qualified to judge abstract commercial cases. He was well placed travelling the western circuit, in parts of which, he liked to say, buggery and bestiality were regarded more as hobbies than crimes, and he did not hear mentioned from one month to the next dry subjects like bills of exchange, or charter parties.

Thea was standing outside the court when the judge's car drew up. Beside her an old man complained that it was not a patch on the old days of assizes, when judges were accompanied by heralds and trumpeters and lords lieutenant. Thea thought that the shiny black car was pompous enough, and knew that the formalities of the judges' lodging were still more than John Withycombe would have chosen. He smiled at her as he went up the steps but did not stop.

Would he, Thea wondered, be relishing this episode?

For nobody could pretend that this court was sitting in its customary manner. The building stood on one side of a cobbled square, and also contained the town hall and the council's administrative offices. There were tubs of flowers and a gaily painted tower. Normally the traffic-free square was used by old age pensioners and young mothers as a convenient resting place, and they sat on the benches and fed the pigeons and seagulls. Today hundreds of students packed the area.

They had been very carefully drilled, for their leaders knew that the authorities would leap at an excuse to end the demonstration; it was illegal to try to influence the administration of justice and nobody could say that they were doing so, for all the banners and posters which had decorated Buriton in the last week were gone. The students stood in neat, almost military formation, and did not chant or call out. One could hardly say that the mere presence outside the court of this crowd of young people was menacing, yet everyone who saw it understood its implication. The message had been delivered in advance.

The judge had already sat for two days in Buriton. It was the far end of the line, and he would have earned his vacation once this list was finished. His marshal, a young woman barrister, looked exhausted, and so did several of the counsel who had been following their briefs around the west country for two months. The judge himself had the same expression of spry interest which had endeared him to the left wing press in the old days, and his own springy black hair straggled out from under the wig, not so much irrepressibly, Thea suspected, as with design.

The jury looked like the magistrates Thea had seen in other courts, representative of the common man, or, since the sexes were mixed, woman.

Thea had left the room when the Crown v Ian Macardle was called. She waited with other witnesses in the entrance hall, tiled and stained-glass decorated, an expression of the stability the students despised. The four students who were there to give evidence looked diminished by the place, though they had defiantly come in jeans and tattered shirts, except for Jenny Pascoe, who was wearing a grey flannel suit with a knee-length skirt.

The noise from outside ceased at the moment that Ian Macardle entered the dock. Thea sat on a bench beside Hubert Dale and they both strained but failed to hear what was being said in the court room. One of the ushers came out and nodded to the young policeman at the door.

'Unlawfully setting fire, Malicious Damage Act 1861, and murder,' he said.

Lewis Rochester arrived later on in the morning, and through the swing doors Thea watched him pace through the silent crowd of students, taller than any of them, and silhouetted in his dark suit against their coloured clothes. He looked into their faces and smiled at some, greeting them by name, and entered the court building looking unworried and at ease; but none of the students answered him, and the four who were waiting to give evidence glanced uneasily at him and went round a corner to sit on the stairs until it was their turn. Jenny too withdrew, though she had greeted him conventionally. Hubert moved nearer Thea, to allow the principal to sit down, but he remained pacing up and down the hall, pausing to read the notices on boards and the gothic inscriptions on the windows. He carried his shoulders so that if he wore a gown it would bell out behind him as he moved. Most academics, Thea thought, hunched into the black stuff of their masters' gowns so that the material clung to the back of their legs.

'What will they do if Ian's sent down for years?' Thea muttered to Hubert; both of them had their eyes on the crowd.

'God knows? Break the place up perhaps? I'm glad I'm not in Rochester's shoes,' he answered.

'Well, he seems self confident enough.'

Hubert was called at this point to give his evidence, about the extent of the damage done to the registry, and the finding of Winston Simpson's body. Thea followed him half an hour later, and went into the witness box literally trembling. She bit on the skin inside her mouth to stop her lips twitching and gripped hard on to the wooden chair.

The usher handed her the Bible and she said, 'I prefer to affirm.' The usher began to ask her reasons, but the judge leant forward, and stopped him. Thea heard a barrister in the well of the court below her whisper, 'He's always soft on troublemakers, our Johnny is.'

Thea described how she had found the manual on explosives in the bookcase in Jenny, Toby and Ian's flat. She hated to do so with Ian Macardle's furious eyes upon her. He was sitting beside a young man with hair like shock-headed Peter, whom Thea recognised from photographs as the president of the National Students' Union. That must be Ian's 'Mackenzie lawyer', the lay adviser to whom anyone was entitled who wished to represent himself without professional help in a court of law. The two young men whispered together as Thea spoke, and then Ian rose to ask her questions. He stood casually, with his hands in his pockets, and with another judge his attempt to antagonise might have succeeded, but John Withycombe claimed to be indifferent to the clothes of the personnel in his court. It had hit the headlines early in the year when he had heard without comment a case presented by a woman barrister wearing not the uniform black skirt, but scarlet trousers. She had told the gossip columnist that she was disappointed at not provoking a reaction. Her gesture had been wasted.

Ian asked Thea hostile and apparently aimless questions about her visit to the flat. He implied that Thea had been acting as an *agent provocateur* and planted the pamphlet, if indeed it was true that it had been in the bookcase at all. But it was only too easy to tell that a Buriton jury would be more likely to believe a professor than poor Ian. It was his word against hers. He had not helped his case by his cross examination, and Thea went to sit at the back of the court room feeling sorry for the boy.

The manual Thea had found was produced and laid on the table. She was followed to the witness stand by a police inspector, who gave evidence about the

166

way the fire started. Arson was first suspected because the blaze appeared to have begun with equal ferocity in three different parts of the building; the registrar's outer office, which contained all the files with applications from prospective students; the principal's own room, and a cloakroom. The barrister mentioned in passing that the principal would testify that he had left his room unlocked that afternoon. The inspector explained how a fire could be started by someone who was at some distance at the time the flames began, with a perfectly common chemical called phosphorus. This was a substance looking like, if his lordship would forgive him, used chewing gum, which was self-igniting if dry; a fire raiser could leave some phosphorus in a perforated container filled with water which would drain slowly away; once the water was gone, the dry phosphorus would warm up and eventually burst into flames, perhaps quarter of an hour after the water had dripped completely away. If such a container were placed under some inflammable curtains, for instance, or under some waste paper, fire would certainly ensue. It was not possible to tell when the container would have been placed in position; so much would depend on the rate of seepage of the water, whether through damp cotton wool, for instance, or dry filter paper. The inspector asked the jury to imagine a coffee percolator.

Some blackened pieces of metal with holes in them were produced at this stage, and the inspector testified that they had been found in the ruins; they were put on the table beside the instruction booklet; the counsel for the prosecution had, of course, read aloud the paragraph in it which described the phosphorus method of starting a fire.

The court adjourned for the day at this point, and Ian was whisked away in a closed van through the crowd of cheering students. But they were quiet again as Rochester made his way through their ranks. Thea went home to tell Sylvester about the day.

'It must have worried Rochester,' she said. 'They were staring at him so—well, I'd have been dead scared. Like animals or something. It would have been much better if they had shouted. But that silence was creepy. The whole damned day was creepy.' She started to cut up meat with some violence. 'I don't think our legal system is all it's cracked up to be. It isn't nice to watch everybody ganging up on one wretched boy. I shan't go again.'

But Sylvester persuaded her to return to court the next morning. He wanted her verbatim report of the proceedings. All the students were there again in formation and silent. It was the best organised demo Thea had seen, and by far the most menacing. But they gave no one an excuse to move them on, and the judge was heard saying in reply to a policeman as he arrived, 'No, no, they have every right—don't interfere.' It cannot have been comfortable standing there, for it was raining and quite cold. The atmosphere in the court was dank.

One could not, Thea realised, think of a much better way of laying out a court room, or of making what was homely to the professional less strange to the layman, for whose benefit, after all, the whole thing existed. But it was unpleasant to see the barristers and ushers so much at ease, and to feel oneself so like a fish out of water. Two barristers were chatting in the aisle beside Thea's seat. She listened to their knowing and sometimes incomprehensible jargon and was irritated by it. Surely dons did not have that certainty that their own professional world was the only one which had objective value? For the lawyers, life began and ended in its relationship to their trade. John Withycombe was being derided because of his unprofessional sympathies; he was too soft, not caring whether laymen respected his court and the majesty of the law, and reluctant to use the sanctions available to preserve his dignity. 'We need some hanging judges back again,' one of them said.

Rochester gave evidence first; he did so precisely and without emotion. The points which he made were firstly, that he had in the last year been shown various types of revolutionary literature which had been floating around the university; secondly, that on the day of the fire he had seen Ian Macardle in his own room in the registry building. They had had an appointment to discuss the demands being made by the students. When asked whether he had left the accused alone at any point, he replied that he had left the room to find a copy of the regulations regarding the admission of students. It had taken him several minutes, as the registrar's room had been locked at the time and the secretary had not been in the outer office.

After much whispering with his friend, Macardle cross examined, but the only point he was able to make was that he had been in the principal's office at the principal's request, which did not get the matter much further since Rochester made the point that he had always tried to be the sort of administrator who heard every side of an argument; in fact that meeting was not the first that he had held with student representatives on the subject of comprehensive tertiary education.

The jury had the glazed look of people who had to force themselves to listen. None of them were making notes, and Thea could not imagine how they could possibly remember what was said over the hours of the trial even if they did understand it. But what would comprehensive tertiary education mean to that obvious farm worker at the back, or the fisherman beside him? And if the smug faced woman in purple knew the phrase, she would reach for her gun. At the beginning of the trial, the papers had told her that morning, Macardle had challenged several jurors, rejecting those who looked most hidebound conventional, but it still looked as though he was faced with a handsome collection of student-haters. There was only one who might have been predisposed in his favour, a bearded schoolmaster type. Thea decided that she hated Buriton, and the legal system, and the smug established world in which she was at home herself.

Ian Macardle was only able to say in his own defence that the evidence was purely circumstantial. It took him a long time to say it, and he produced several witnesses, including Jenny and Toby, to the fact that he had often spoken against the use of violence. He showed that the pamphlet about explosions could have been left in his bookcase by any number of people, for the three of them kept open house. Not only their friends came there, after all; even the principal himself had been in the room, when he once brought Jenny back in his car. But how could he prove that he had not taken phosphorus from laboratories which were open to any member of the university? How, on the other hand, could the prosecution prove that he had? Nor did the fact that he could have left an explosive device in the registry building mean that he had done so.

The judge left his summing up until after the lunch break. He spoke in a quiet, reflective voice, addressing the jurors as though they were at his dinner table, and they seemed, for the first time, to be responsive people, nodding and even smiling at his remarks. He said nothing which could be extracted from the speech and held against him, but the effect was utterly in favour of acquitting Ian Macardle; there was sufficient evidence for the jury to consider, but the judge himself was clearly not convinced by it.

Thea heard the two barristers in front of her, and watched them shake their heads and close up their files in a way that another judge than John Withycombe might have objected to. 'He's just telling them to let him off,' one of them muttered audibly.

Having dealt with the evidence about fire raising, the judge came to the question of the murder charge. There was no doubt, he told the jury, that the death of Winston Simpson had been caused by the fire, and that whoever started the fire had caused his death. But it could only be murder, if that person had known that Simpson might be killed as a result. Whether he intended him to die, or had merely foreseen that he might, it would be murder. And, the judge went on, the jury had heard evidence that it was common knowledge amongst the student body that Winston Simpson was living in the registry building, and that he frequently spent the afternoon in a drugged stupor in his room.

On the other hand, the judge added, the jury might think that the very fact that the accused knew that Simpson was there made it unlikely that he would put him motivelessly in such danger.

It took the jury two hours to reach their verdict: Guilty of the first charge, not guilty of murder. Thea was irreverently reminded of the definition of a camel: a horse designed by a committee. Obviously the jurors who wanted him guilty of both charges had done a deal with those who wanted to acquit entirely, and they had agreed to compromise. She quickly wiped the smile from her lips. It was no laughing matter, and John Withycombe was distressed, as even those who did not know him must be able to see.

At this stage, Ian's counsel if he had one, would have made a plea in mitigation, but Ian Macardle refused to beg for any mercy. The prosecuting barrister asked whether he might help: there were no previous convictions but the principal of the university would like to give character evidence.

Rochester returned to the stand.

'Thank you, your honour, for giving me the opportunity,' he said. 'I should like to say that Ian Macardle must by definition be a public spirited young man; he has always concerned himself with the affairs of the student body and been active in university affairs. He comes, I believe, from a comfortable background, but not a rich one. His father was a traffic controller with an omnibus company, though both his parents died recently. He was educated at a state grammar school, and of course receives a grant to be at the university.'

'You want to ask the court to be lenient with this promising student?' the judge said, almost hopefully.

'If I may have the indulgence of the court, I would like to say a little more.' Rochester, standing self-confidently in the witness box, might have been in command of the room.

'Please go on.'

'Your honour, you will no doubt expect to hear me say that Macardle would have his career ruined by excessive punishment, and that the state should not add its severity to the suffering which having his studies curtailed will cause.' Rochester hooked his thumbs behind his lapels, and got well into his stride. 'Your honour, this is, I contend, a mistaken view. The very fact that students are privileged to receive the benefits of higher education should render them the more deserving of punishment when they transgress the codes of behaviour to which those who provide their education subscribe. They should, to put it simply, know better.'

'Mr Rochester,' the judge interrupted. 'Specifically with regard to Ian Macardle, I should be glad to hear your comments; this is not the place for general speculation.'

'As your honour pleases. In that case, I merely wish to say that as far as his position as a student is concerned, I do not ask that the rigours of the law should be mitigated.'

There was a growing murmuring sound from the crowd outside. Hubert Dale was sitting beside Thea this afternoon. He had started to rise when Rochester first spoke, but sank back on to the seat with a muffled groan, and listened with his head clasped in his hands. 'God, won't the press just make hay with this,' he said bitterly.

'It sounds as though the students outside are getting it relayed,' Thea said.

'Yes, the crowd's getting ugly. What on earth did he want to go and say that for?'

'Silence in court,' an usher called. John Withycombe looked angry in a way that Thea had not seen. He said curtly, 'I'll adjourn until a social enquiry report can be made. The court will rise.' He marched from the room.

Hubert and Thea went into the entrance hall; framed by the double doors, a section of the square outside could be seen; the students had relaxed their control, and were all now moving and shouting, and some had produced banners saying 'Release Macardle Now' and other similar messages. They stood grudgingly aside to let the legal staff come through, and the policemen, though at the ready, were not needed. Thea said sharply, 'Come on Hubert, you're not afraid of them are you?' and went firmly out into the drizzling cold. Rochester's words were being repeated, and suddenly his very voice sounded amplified; someone had smuggled a cassette recorder in, and was now broadcasting the principal's words.

A high girl's voice cried, 'Lynch him!' and it was followed by a chant which grew rapidly in volume, of 'Rochester out, Rochester out'. The principal had not appeared on the steps yet; a man called, 'He's escaping the back way,' and some of the people at the edges of the crowd ran off to find the other exit from the court.

Then a familiar voice from the top of the steps called, 'Hey, listen, listen to me.' Toby Norman had just come out, and was standing there holding his hands out to silence the crowd. Gradually the noise died away, and Toby Norman spoke as he had so often done.

'You can't do anything to him,' he said.

'Why not? Let's do him in!'

'Who was that? Ken, was that you? Well, listen. What do we want anyway? The whole point is, what we were working for, was for all our mates to get the chances we get. Right?'

'What's that got to do with Rochester?'

'Nothing, don't you see, he's not the point. OK, so he's a fascist, but that's not the point. But Ian's only had the treatment that other kids get. We're all in it together ...' Toby went on for a little while, soothing the crowd more by magic than logic, but soothed they were, and a few minutes later, when Rochester came out of the court, the students let

175

him pass through untouched, and followed by only a few hostile growls. And as he passed Toby Norman, he thanked him very warmly.

CHAPTER TEN

The physiotherapist said that I was a slow learner;
she was a hearty and healthy girl, strong as a shire
horse, who had been trained to stand no nonsense,
and knew better than I did what hurt me, and was
unmoved by my pleas to consider the prohibitions
on exertion which had guarded my last few months.
She gave no quarter in the fight to teach me to use
crutches. My arm muscles hurt more than my leg
had ever done, after a couple of sessions with her,
but she persevered and made me persevere, and by
the end of the week I was nipping around the ground
floor feeling quite spry, and had learnt the theory
of climbing stairs. But there wasn't much to go up
and down for. Tim Gifford wanted me to get some
fresh air, but it rained relentlessly and I wasn't eager.

Thea went back to work for the last week of term.
Ian Macardle was given an unusually light sentence
in spite of Rochester's widely reported appeal for
punishment; now that the matter was no longer *sub
judice*, a national controversy raged as to whether a
year in an open prison was adequate for arson, with
predictable battle lines drawn up, the bring-back-

hanging brigade against the professional letter signers of the left. My interest in the discussion was sharpened by Thea quoting a remark of John Withycombe's after the trial, that he was certain that Ian Macardle had nothing to do with the fire at all.

Toby Norman, or the conviction of Ian, or perhaps just the ending of the term, had taken the heat out of the situation in Buriton. Thea reported that the students she saw were meek and industrious.

With unprecedented speed, the district council had granted planning permission to Desmond Pascoe's consortium, and the town council had conveyed the lease of Freeman's Common; bulldozers and earth movers were already chewing up the grass and daffodils.

On the last day of term, Rochester announced to the assembled senate of the university, that he had been offered and had accepted the vice chancellorship of the Northern University.

I felt restless; the sun was shining from time to time between showers, and the room seemed dusty and irritating. Thea was out shopping. I swung myself into the hall, and stood looking up the stairs. I'd been up and down them with the physiotherapist, balancing my heavy body on the crutches, terrified at each step that the rubber would slip and I should fall and break the other leg. The steps rose in a gentle curve, carpeted in yellow haircord, with curly black iron banisters.

I sat on the bottom step, and tried heaving myself

upwards on my bottom. It worked well, and I took the crutches up with me, grimacing at the feeling of the haircord on my blistered hands, and the soreness where the crutches had rubbed under my arms. I hadn't even been into the first floor room, and was surprised when I looked in the door now to see our own furniture from the house in London huddled in the middle of the floor. It would have made a pretty drawing-room, L-shaped, with long windows to open on to a small balcony, and a marble fire place. In one corner was our old dining table, spread with papers and files: Thea's desk.

The second flight of stairs was narrower and steeper, and wearied me intensely to ascend. I had not even realised—not that I'd thought about it—that the house was on three floors. The sun was shining through a cupola in the roof. Clovis' room and Thea's conventional bedroom with the single bed neatly made; how tidy she kept it, when my belongings didn't have to share the space. The third room was full of boxes and old chairs, and among them my own dusty luggage.

I wedged myself into an old armchair, and opened the first case. It felt like looking through the relics of someone who had died. Where was the man who had set off with his equipment to the Far East? Not here. Without the slightest sensation of ownership I recognised the notebook filled with my own handwriting, the checked spongebag with which I had travelled since my schooldays, the volume of Proust through which I intended to force myself in lonely hotels. There was a photograph of Clovis aged two running towards the camera, and the same snap shot of Thea which appeared on the dust jacket of her popular books. The baggage had only reached Buriton recently, sent on at last from whatever recesses of an eastern police station it had lain in since last year, and when it had come Thea hadn't managed to interest me in unpacking it. It depressed me now to glance at the notes and sketches I had made.

I emptied my open brief case upside down on to my lap; the papers scattered, sliding under furniture. I would not want them again. The little gun fell on to my knee.

I'd forgotten the weapon. Bernard had slipped it into my pocket as he said goodbye, more like one of Clovis's toys than anything else. I'd laughed, but he said, 'Take it, dear boy, take it. You never know when you may be glad of it. Look, it holds these,' and he handed me a small packet of ammunition.

'Stick 'em up,' I said, embarrassed, trying to give it back, but he insisted I should keep it, and in the end I packed it under the spare batteries for my razor and the box of extra typewriter ribbons. The idea seemed ridiculous and melodramatic, and I forgot that I had the thing. I dare say it would have been detected at Heathrow, but I went up to Scotland to say goodbye to my mother before I flew, and at Aberdeen the checks were perfunctory. I fiddled with the absurd little object. It should probably be handed in to the police. I dropped it in my pocket. The little room was stuffy, and I pushed up the window, and leant out. The air outside smelt fresh and spring like, and dinghies were sailing in the bay. Children played traditionally on the pavement and at the edges of the common. The palm trees were shiny and burgeoning after a winter of looking like dusty refugees. In the house next door, the old lady was hanging out a sign which offered bed and breakfast.

When Jenny walked by she looked almost furtively at the house, as though she hoped that I would not see her, but I called and she came up.

'Actually, I'm glad to see you today,' she said in a social voice. 'I wondered whether you might give me a reference?'

'What for?'

'A secretarial job or something. Perhaps a receptionist.'

'For the vacation, do you mean?'

'No, I'm leaving the university.'

'They're not sending you down?'

'Not that I know of. But I've had enough. What's the good of it?'

'What about the baby?'

'I'm not pregnant after all. It was a mistake. Mistakes do happen!' she added, defensively.

'So why not finish, get your degree?'

'Oh, Sylvester, I've grown out of it. It's all so pointless, what is there in it for me—all that sitting around in rags and talk talk talking?'

'You used not to think like that,' I said sadly. She looked worldly and conventional. She had become commonplace, my Jenny, the sort of girl who came by the dozen.

'I'm grown up, that's all. All that chatter doesn't get anyone anywhere, does it? I've been a little nit.'

181

'Perhaps you're—um, moving northwards?' I suggested.

'Northwards? Oh, you mean—no. I'm not. I'm living at home with mum. Dad has moved out. And I've met Barry. That's my—well, you know. He works in the hotel business.' The front door banged below, and a deep voice called,

'Sylvester? Anyone in?'

'Up here,' I answered. Jenny and I waited in silence while the heavy footsteps climbed. Lewis Rochester put his head round the door.

'My dear fellow—good to see you getting about. Good morning, Jenny. How are you?'

'Very well, thank you.' She spoke primly, her eyes on the ground. 'I must go. Goodbye, Sylvester. Professor Rochester.'

Rochester hardly waited until she was out of the room before saying, 'Wasn't there some story about her being pregnant? Had an abortion, I suppose.'

'They were saying it was your baby,' I said.

'Mine?' He laughed barkingly. 'I wouldn't have minded getting in there, I can tell you, but I drew back at the brink, as you might say. A student at one's own university . . . I may have broadened her mind, but I didn't touch her, I'm sorry to say. Pretty girl.' We watched her running up the street. Her silky hair flopped up and down on her back.

'She used to be more than pretty,' I said. 'She had a kind of purity.'

'Purity! My dear fellow, she's been living with Tobias Norman and our local fire raiser.'

'I wasn't meaning sexual innocence.'

'What else is there? She's just grown up, that's all. You don't want to worry too much about a girl like that, there are too many of them. Bright enough to get the A levels, but really made for reproducing the species. They go through these phases, being unconventional, flouting all the rules their mothers taught them—but it passes off, mercifully. I've seen her once or twice this term. If I've helped to speed the maturing process—'

'You taught her cynicism?'

'It's part of my job. They can't go through life all starry eyed. Though did she have ideals, would you say, or merely instincts?'

I thought, he changed her life and he doesn't even remember it. But should I count him guilty of destroying her principles when he could not recognise them?

There were some boys kicking a ball round on the pavement. I used to play football on Primrose Hill with Clovis. I ached to kick the rigid leather. I shifted uneasily.

'Anything wrong? Shall I help you downstairs?'

'No thanks. I'll go down later.'

We stood side by side at the window. A group of students passed down the road carrying cases and haversacks. 'They look quite peaceful now,' I said.

'Well, they have had their fling. Till the next time. But I expect my successor will be putty in their hands.'

'As you were not?'

'It's all a question of psychology, my dear chap.

183

Look at their occupation, as they called it, of the university buildings. Nobody suffered except the students themselves. Once they had realised that, it all faded away. And they'll have to pay to make good the damage out of union funds.'

'Will they?'

'If it's that or no degree next term. You see, they know that I mean what I say.'

'And you won't be here to suffer for it.'

'That too,' he admitted. 'Or,' he added, waving his hand at the bulldozers, 'for that.'

'So you win. And who loses?'

He looked injured, and then said, cocking an eyebrow at me, 'Nobody. Joyce gets Desmond Pascoe—you knew that, I think—Pascoe gets his developer's profits, Buriton gets what it deserves.'

'And the students?'

'Get a dose of hard work. I'd say I've done quite well.'

'You make yourself sound positively public spirited.'

'Oh, I am. After all, it's the duty of those of us who are able and intelligent to use our qualities to direct the rest along the right path.'

'You once drew another conclusion, I remember. You said that it was the duty of the intelligent to reproduce themselves—have a lot of children.'

'I'd say there's no doubt about that. When you look at the great mass of people, the lumpen proletariat, you realise that they don't—or can't—think. They direct their nerve endings from the bowel. No it's damned few of us who can wish to live by the brain. I sometimes fancy that we're here as guardians; shepherds of the sheep.'

'Sheep?'

'Yes, compared with those of us who have a higher brain power. How would the world manage without people like us? Take universities, a world in minia-ture, full of scholars who have no more common sense than a coal heaver. The whole fabric of society, or of our little society here, would break down with-out a strong man to direct affairs.'

'You feel that a man like you has a divine call to petty kingship?' I said.

'Well—in a way perhaps. I'd describe it as a duty more than a right. Even for monarchs, as Elizabeth the Great said, the crown is a more glorious thing to them that see it than those that bear it. No, the burden of office must fall upon those with strong enough backs not to break under it. And those are the people with superior intellect.'

'Who are often very impractical persons.'

'Oh, no, my dear fellow, that's folklore. The absent minded professor is a creature of fiction. Or if he's all that absent minded, he isn't all that intelligent. If you are superior in one field you are capable of leadership in others, and of organising things for the best.'

'The victims *nolentes volentes*?'

'Willy nilly? Well—' Thea came into the room with a couple of glasses of sherry. She was flushed from the sunshine outside, and pretty, and exuded intelligence without any illusions of her own mem-bership of a race of *übermenschen*. Yet she sparkled at Rochester, and he held her hand too long in his.

'Are you moving soon, Lewis?' she said. Since when did she call him by his first name?

'They are doing up the vice chancellor's house for me. I'll pick up the reins by next term.'

'Leaving all our troubles behind you,' she reproached him, ironically.

'All sorted out, my dear. The young have lost their ringleaders.'

'It was funny about Toby Norman,' Thea said. 'Someone was saying today that he always went round with Ian. That time he came to see you in the registry building, on the day of the fire, was Ian really alone then? They used to be like Siamese twins.'

'I gave evidence that I saw Ian only,' Rochester answered.

'Just as well for the other one. He's already in America, I hear.'

'It would have been a tragedy for the Normans if he had failed to get a visa. Apart from this peace mission frolic, which of course he'll grow out of, they have considerable property in Virginia, as you know.'

'But Toby would never have lied for the sake of—?' Thea looked genuinely distressed.

Rochester shrugged, and moved to look out of the window. He said, 'There's your son coming.'

'I'll go down.' I heard Thea go into her bedroom, and then down the stairs.

'I must be off,' Rochester said. He loomed above me, self assured and arrogant. Perhaps the complicated fabric of our society needs men who know themselves to be invaluable to it. The very qualities which made me hate him might be those which would best serve his academic community.

'Did the duchess persuade you to shield her boy?' I asked.

He looked surprised, and then smiled intimately. He stood leaning against the window, framed by its alcove, his hands in his pockets.

'I have known the family for some time,' he said. 'Such a pity if the boy ruined his life for a nonsense —don't you agree?'

'And Toby agreed to the deception?'

'Sins of omission, my dear fellow ... and we put it to him sensibly. He's grown up a little, I think—which is what the university is there for, after all.'

'The omission being that he refrained from telling the authorities that he never left Ian Macardle's side?'

'They wouldn't have believed him in any case. It would have been an obvious sacrifice in the cause of friendship.'

'Not if it was true,' I said. He looked at me thoughtfully, without answering. 'What about Macardle?' I said. 'Was he there?'

'Oh, he was there all right. There was an appointment to see me. The truth was told, my dear Sylvester, even if not quite the whole truth.'

'Toby won't be able to live with himself, after doing that,' I said.

'He can't live on theories for ever. Reality breaks in.'

'You put it to him straight, did you?' I asked

savagely, and he nodded. 'I suppose you started the fire too, now that we are speaking frankly?'

'No comment, even off the record,' he said. He was still smiling. He knew that he was safe in private with me, ill and a little mad as I was well known to be.

'Why? Just to use the site for building? Did you buy off Desmond Pascoe with it?'

'You won't provoke me, Sylvester. I've proved I'm a strong man, after all,' he said.

'Oh. Now I see it. With Toby leading the student demonstrators they were too peaceful for your liking —is that it? They never broke the law, not even a moral law, they never broke anything, he kept them close to passive resistance. They used sweet reason, and you couldn't show the world how well you handled them because they slithered from your grasp? And the Northern University wants a strong man. So if they wouldn't be violent you did it for them. I suppose you'd planned it for whenever they marched. And it had been well advertised. You knew fine when it would be. So you summoned the leaders to an appointment earlier in the day, and then planted the explosive yourself. And later you left the pamphlet in Ian's flat, when you were taking Jenny home. Am I right?'

He didn't answer, but smiled tolerantly. He didn't look at all worried.

'What about those two boys, Rochester? Macardle behind bars, and Winston Simpson dead? I suppose you didn't know he was there. Only the students knew that. It was a campus joke against the staff.

188

Even you wouldn't have killed him.' That stung him. He said,

'You don't understand me at all. I'd have killed Simpson without thinking twice about it, though in fact I did not know that he was in the registry building. But if you can see my design, surely then you accept the motives? If a drug soaked drop-out died, does it matter in comparison with the good I can do? Have you any idea of the position of the head of a university like the Northern? I'll have influence on the development of education for the next fifty years, I'll shape the future. And the country needs people with the vision and the ability for the job. If a youth who has rendered himself sub-human with self administered poisons dies five years earlier in the process—or a conceited working class boy spends a year digging potatoes in an open prison, does it matter? They aren't useful to society, they don't contribute. They are dross, not worth a second thought, gooks.'

He was looking out of the window. That word pressed into my mind in the same way as the gun's hard metal pressed into my hand. I gazed at this corrupted, corrupting man, and remembered Toby's and Ian's idealism, before they came into contact with him, and how Jenny had admired him. I thought of Clovis, still unmoulded by life, and of Thea, who had liked this man. I thought of those massacred peasants, whose killers had called them gooks.

Even in this country I have heard the call for tougher laws and orders, stronger obedience and loyalty, for the emergence of a forceful leader. Even I have undervalued a single conscience and mocked an unconforming conviction. I've lived in what we call civilisation and acquiesced in it. This man made dissenters assent; but when I die, the memory of compliance will not comfort me.

And so, dear Reader, dear Esmond and Bernard, dear Clovis, dear—above all, dear Thea, and so, I murdered him.